I Wish I Was a Cowboy

Wayne Simmes

Published by Wayne Simmes, 2022.

I WISH I WAS A COWBOY

First edition. September 2, 2022.

ISBN: 979-8215099094

Written by Wayne Simmes.

Title Page
I Wish I Was a Cowboy
Wayne Simmes
Copyright 2015
Smashwords Edition

I Wish I Was a Cowboy

Part One

Chapter One – One Door Closes

William Anderson knew he was dying. It was not because of the pain but rather the lack thereof. For the past five years, there had never been a day when he was absent of pain. Oh, in the beginning, the drugs had worked fairly well but as time progressed and as cancer spread no amount of pain medication could dampen it enough so that he was comfortable. But today he had awoken and the pain was gone. He knew that was his body's way of telling him that it had had enough and that it was ready to shut down.

He was not a man afraid of death. He had reconciled a long time ago that death was just the end of the natural order of things. He did not believe that he was going to heaven or the opposite place. He was reasonably sure that there was no God, loving or otherwise as he had seen proof of God's absence throughout his life.

He thought back to just a few days ago when his ex-wife had come for a final visit. She was determined that in his last and final days that she could convince him to make a reconciliation with the God she so loved and adored. It was her belief in God and his lack of belief that had led them to the divorce court, but now she was sure that she could change Will's mind. After all had she not heard the old saying, "there are no atheists in foxholes," many times? When a man or a woman came face to face with the reality of final judgment most if not all decide to reconcile with their maker. And she was positive that Will would be no different.

And so she had come to call and she brought her minister as a backup. Surely Will would listen to a man of the cloth if not to her.

As she entered the room and saw the man she had lived with for more than half of her life she felt a rush of empathy for him. She could tell he was near his final breath and she went to his bedside and took his hand in hers.

"You know I still love you, Will?"

"I have never doubted that for a minute, Amy? I just wished we could have worked out our differences in the past. Now I am afraid that it is too late."

"Will it is never too late to make amends. I brought Reverend Williams with me today to help you to make amends with God."

"Amy I thought we were talking about you and me. You know I have no faith in a higher power. And while Mr. Williams is welcome in my house, I certainly do not want him trying to convert me to a religion that I find to be hypocritical."

"Will, why do you have to be so stubborn? Surely you have to realize that there is a loving God that created all things."

"Where was your loving God hiding while millions of people died of AIDS? Was their suffering a sign of his love?"

Reverend Williams stepped forward and took Will's other hand. "We do not know everything about God's ways. Perhaps there is a greater reason for those people's suffering. Perhaps it is God's way of telling them to repent from their wicked ways."

"So your loving God was so vindictive that he not only allowed a new and terrible disease to be created by some man-made organization but he used it to punish millions of people? And before you go any further and try to convince me that all those people were sinners, please remember that a great many of the victims were children. Many of those contracted AIDS in their mother's wombs. And how about all the Jews that Hitler gassed during the Second World War? Why did God allow that to happen? Why did he not step in and protect those people?"

"Will, all people are God's children. Which ones do you think he should destroy?"

"It seems pretty clear to me that the Nazis were the evil ones. If there was a God, he should have put a stop to those maniacs."

And so the argument had waged. No one made any real headway as both sides were firmly entrenched in their positions. And finally, Amy had thrown up her hands in a gesture of defeat and had pronounced that Will was going straight to hell unless he repented at the last hour.

Well, the last hour, or nearly so, was upon him and Will had no thoughts of repentance. Sure he knew that he had not led a perfect life. He had told his share of lies, either to avoid some unpleasantness or to spare the feelings of others. He chuckled as he thought of how many poorly cooked meals he had eaten just to avoid telling Amy that she might need some instruction in the culinary arts. But by and large, Will figured he had dealt fairly with his fellow man. And he had gone out of his way to help others whenever he could. So even if he was wrong about the existence of God, which he was sure he was not, he was sure he was not destined for a life of eternal torment.

Normally he had instructed those in charge of his care to leave the lights on. He had no trouble sleeping in a lit room and he figured he would spend enough time in darkness later. But tonight he wanted to fade away with the light. And as dusk settled across the room he let his mind wander to his happy place. A place of open ranges, of lowing cattle and loyal horses. He had always loved the idea of being a cowboy; he had just been born about a hundred years too late.

And as the last vestiges of light left the room it left his eyes for the last time as well. Will Anderson no longer existed.

Chapter Two - A New Beginning

Few of us have ever known total darkness unless, of course, we are completely blind. Almost everywhere we are there is some degree of light. Perhaps it is in the form of the moon or stars, or perhaps a street light shining through a window, or the never-ending incessant glow of LEDs from clocks, radios, cable boxes, or digital recorders.

So when Will awoke to total and complete darkness he was surprised. He checked to his right to where his bedside clock should be but it was not there. He looked to his left where the display from his cable box should be but it too was missing. He reached for the button that was constantly by his hand to call for the nurse but no button was to be found.

Now he started to become alarmed. Where exactly was he? Something heavy was across his arms and body. Certainly, it was too heavy to be his comforter and sheets. He had become used to the lack of movement but he finally tried to throw off whatever was covering him. It was heavy but was not difficult to move once he found the edge.

Once his arms were free he reached out to try and determine where he was. He quickly realized that he was not in his bed or any bed because his arms were level with a hard cold surface. He must be laying on some kind of rock or cement surface and he began to wonder if he had not been placed in some kind of burial crypt. If so they must have mistaken him for being dead and buried him alive. But that did not make sense to him because he had no such crypt nor did he know of anyone in his family that did.

Finally realizing that he could not see even a few feet away from him, he tried to hone in on his other senses. The first thing he noticed was that it was very cold where he was and he reached for the edge of what had been covering him and pulled it closer to his body. He then tried to listen for some sound that might be around him and he was surprised to note that somewhere close there was a dripping sound like water falling but not quite like a leaky faucet.

His next effort was to try and smell what might be in his immediate surroundings. He took several large intakes of breath. There was an odor that was vaguely familiar to him, one that he should easily recognize from somewhere in his past. It was not an unpleasant odor although it was somewhat musky. He now suspected that perhaps he was not alone. That somewhere close by there was an animal of some kind. And so he suspected that instead of being in a crypt perhaps he was in some kind of cave.

That thought was almost as frightening as being buried alive because of what kind of animals live in caves. The first thought was that bears live in caves. He had never been close to a bear so he could not tell if the odor he detected could be from such an animal or not. But the smell was far too familiar for that.

He thought back to his childhood days on a farm in Western, New York State, and the odors that he remembered from those days. It surely was not cattle. They had a much ranker smell. And then it hit him. What he smelled was the odor of a horse. But what in the name of the great horned ghost would a horse be doing in a cave and with him no doubt?

This had to be some kind of dream although not an unpleasant one so he curled back under his warm covering and allowed his mind to rest. How much time elapsed he had no way of knowing. But at some point, he heard what he knew was a horse nickering and he rolled from under what he could now see to be some kind of animal hide. There was a faint light that illuminated his surroundings enough to be able to tell that he was in fact inside a cave of some kind. And he could see the outline of a horse not too far from where he lay. He rolled completely out from under the hide and surveyed what he could see of his body. He certainly was not dressed in pajamas as he had been for the last several months. Instead, he had a checkered heavy shirt and blue jeans and on his feet were pointed boots.

"Wow, this is a great dream," he thought. "I always wanted to be a cowboy and here I am right down to the cowboy boots and horse."

He then saw that the light was rapidly increasing. He could now clearly see his surroundings and was surprised to note that next to where he lay was a holstered handgun and against the wall of the cave nearly within his reach was a rifle. And even more surprising was the fact that he recognized both weapons as guns that he had owned in the past. He could also see the horse now and was shocked that he also recognized the horse as one he had ridden hundreds of times in his youth. Now he knew that this was a dream but it certainly was the most vivid dream he had ever had.

"Well, I might as well get the most out of this dream," he thought. And so he got to his feet and started towards the source of the light. He had only gone a few feet when he came to a bend in the wall and following around it he saw the mouth of the cave and the sunlight beyond. He made his way outside and saw that he was on a ledge of a rock wall. A few feet away was a worn path that was perhaps wide enough for a horse and rider but steep enough so that it might not be safe to ride the horse down it.

The sun was nearly over the horizon across what he observed was a deep valley. The air was extremely cold, but not the bone-numbing cold of winter. It was more like early spring when you have hopes that when the sun has fully emerged from its hiding place there is the hope of warmth. He wrapped his arms tightly across his chest trying to keep what little body heat he might have inside. He knew that the intelligent thing would be to retreat into the cave and find the animal hide and wrap his body back inside it. But he was too intrigued by trying to find out what his purpose in this dream could be.

He carefully scanned the horizon and was somewhat surprised to note that for miles in all directions he saw no signs of civilization. There were no power lines or highways. He could hear no sounds indicating that automobiles or trucks were passing on some nearby road. Certainly, there were places like this on earth but they were becoming fewer and fewer as the encroachment of man grew. He then looked upward to the now well-illuminated sky. No matter where he looked he could see no jet trails. And the sky was as clear and blue as he had ever seen. There was no sign of pollution of any kind. It was almost as if he had been transferred back to a time before the industrial revolution.

Satisfied that he had seen what he could in his immediate area, he went back into the cave to see what else had been provided for him. The first thing he found and was extremely grateful for was a denim jacket. He put it on and was pleased that it was a perfect fit. He looked all around him and spied two saddlebags. They were large and when he picked them up he noticed that they were quite heavy as well. Pulling on the leather strap that secured one of the bags, he looked inside. There was a change of clothes including socks and underwear and what appeared to be some kind of beef jerky that was not wrapped in anything. And on the bottom of the bag, he found hundreds of rounds of ammunition for two different weapons.

"Now, I wonder why I would need all that fire power. Am I some kind of soldier or perhaps a lawman of sorts? Or maybe I am an outlaw on the run from the law? Or maybe I am just plain crazy."

Chapter Three - Time to Explore

Seeing that his canteens were nearly empty, he figured it was time to explore the great outdoors. He reached down and picked up his gun belt and strapped it on and then like the gunfighter of old tied it down to his leg and removed the hammer strap. Picking up his canteens with his left hand he made his way out of the cave entrance and to the trail that he had seen earlier. It was indeed narrow and steep and he had to keep constant watch of his step. But after a few yards, it began to level out and widen out as well. There were tall bushes on either side of the trail and once he scared a rabbit from under a bush, which set his heart aflutter. He had gone probably a quarter-mile when he saw an indentation off to his left. He stopped and studied the area and he could see that the vegetation was growing taller and greener. He suspected that meant that there was a source of water close by and since that was what he was looking for he began to angle in that direction.

There definitely was a path through the bushes. Apparently, game frequented the area and used this route to the water hole. The trail began to widen out as if whatever animals used this route would become in a hurry and spread out. And then he saw it; a spring set into the rocks and water spilling out and down the mountainside. From the speed of the flow, he was sure that this water would be cold and sweet. He had nearly reached the spring when something told him there was danger. He heard the sound before he saw the snake but he was almost upon it by that time. Everything slowed down to a crawl. He planted his foot to stop and he could see the coils on the deadly snake constricting. The head came back and launched forward. He knew that he was going to be bitten but the strangest thing happened. Before the snake could strike him he saw the head separate from the body and fly away in a bloody mist. It was only then that he heard the roar of a pistol. He immediately looked around to see who it was that had miraculously come to his rescue, but he saw no one.

This seemed almost impossible for he knew that whoever had shot that snake had to be extremely close. Now that his heart had slowed down to a semi-normal level, he could even smell the cordite in the air. Only then did he look directly down and realize that his pistol was in his hand. He tilted the muzzle up close to his nose and he could tell that his weapon had just been fired.

"This is nuts," he thought. "On my best day, I could not have made that shot." He had practiced long hours with a pistol and was fairly accurate with one but only if he took his time and a two-handed stance. Quickdraw was not his forte. But somehow he knew that just this once he had been deadly fast and accurate. Worried that there might be more than one snake, he kicked the dead body out of his path and carefully made his way to the water. Taking a long stick he began beating the bushes around the water hole until he was satisfied that any other reptiles would have slithered away. He then put his revolver back in the holster and bent down and filled both canteens to the brim.

He thought about taking the dead snake with him and trying to cook it, but he had no idea how to dress a snake. And he suspected that trying to google the answer in that cave or near it would not be possible.

He carefully made his way back to the top of the path, took his canteens into the cave, poured a generous portion of water into his hat, and gave it to the horse. "So what am I going to call you, old friend? You look like you might be aristocracy, so I think I will call you Prince. Come along then let's see if we can find you a royal meal."

He had heard many times that it was a fool that holstered an empty gun and he figured that he should reload the cartridge that he had spent on the snake. So he took out his pistol and popped open the cylinder and removed the spent brass. He carefully put the empty in his pocket as he did not know if he would need to find someone to reload the rounds or if he could just purchase new ones. Satisfied that he had a full revolver he grabbed the horse's lead rope and led him from the cave. He did not like the idea of leading the horse down the steep incline but he saw no alternative. He just hoped that he could keep his footing and stay ahead of the horse. Being run over by his animal would turn the dream into a nightmare.

The horse was much more sure-footed than he would have imagined and soon they were at the stage where the trail leveled and widened out. He now wished that he had taken the time to saddle the animal but he was not planning on going too far in any event. He had passed the water hole and was soon in a flat area on the side of the hill, which was covered, in lush green grass. Somehow he trusted the horse not to run away and he dropped the lead rope to the ground and allowed Prince to graze. In the meantime, he also felt the pangs of hunger and wondered when he might have eaten last. He began to scour the area and before long he came upon a thick patch of blackberries. He removed his hat and began to pick the ripe fruit into it. It did not take long before he had the hat about a quarter-way full and he stopped picking. He certainly was not going to make a pie and so anything beyond what he planned to eat would just go to waste.

He sat down on a fallen log and began to enjoy the bounty that nature had provided him. He did know however that if he were to survive he would have to have something more than berries to eat. As he surveyed his surroundings he noticed that some ways down the slope it appeared there was some type of hardwood forest. He figured that there might be game to be had there and thought about retreating to the cave to retrieve the rifle he had seen earlier. Checking the position of the sun he knew that the day was over half gone and by the time he retreated to the cave and got down the hill dusk would be upon him. For today the berries and some of the jerky he had seen in his saddlebags would have to do. He would start at first light tomorrow and see what he could hunt up. As he was musing on this he felt something gently nudge him in the back. Startled he looked around and then chuckled for Prince was pushing him with his nose.

"Ok old friend," he said. "I guess you think it is time to head back as well. We will get a good night's rest and then head out in the morning for a more thorough look around."

By the time they had returned to the cave, the sun had almost set behind the hill. Will figured he would have enough light to at least gather some wood for a fire. There were no large trees in the area but there was plenty of dead brush. He was careful as he gathered it, as he did not want a repeat encounter with a snake. He knew he was just lucky that morning and was pretty sure he would not be so fortunate again. With a large armful of wood, he entered the cave and began looking for a place where he could build a fire without smoking Prince and himself out. He found some matches at the bottom of his saddlebag and made himself a makeshift torch which he lit. He walked towards the back of the cave and noticed that the smoke was drawn further inside the cave. He figured there must be a natural chimney close by and simply followed the smoke. In a short time, he found the place he was looking for. There was a ready-made pit where someone before his visit here had made a fire of their own. He retreated to the cave entrance and brought the armload of brush back to the pit and started a fire. He was pleased to note that the smoke drifted upward and that the fire gave some light throughout the cave.

At the first sign of morning light, Will saddled Prince and loaded his supplies. He did not leave anything behind, as he had no reason to return to the cave. He did not know how long this dream would last but he saw no reason to spend it in one place. There must be more interesting places to be than inside a cave. He led the horse down to the spring, keeping a close eye out for snakes. He filled the canteens and allowed Prince to drink his fill and then mounted the horse and started down the mountain. He made better time riding than he had the previous day leading the horse and soon he was at the edge of the forest he had spotted yesterday.

This was an older growth of trees and the limbs above almost blocked out the sun. Will saw no signs of logging or other man-made activity such as brush piles. In a few places where the trees had died of a natural cause or because they had been struck by lightning, the forest opened up and allowed lower vegetation to grow. As he rode he kept an eye out for any game that might be found. Once he saw the white tail of a deer disappearing in the trees ahead but he was not looking for something that large. He knew that if he shot a deer the vast majority of the meat would go to waste.

As the day wore on both horse and rider were grateful when they finally came out into a large meadow with a fast-moving creek meandering down the center. The rider dismounted and led his horse to the water and allowed him to drink his fill. While that was taking place Will refilled what he had used from his canteens. One never knows how long it will be before you find water again in a strange land. He surveyed the sky and again was amazed at how blue and unmarked by any signs of air travel. Surely there were very few places on earth where planes did not leave their trail in the sky. He also noted that the sun was rapidly making its way toward the skyline. He needed to find a place to make camp for the night and hopefully find something to supplement his diet.

He removed the bridle from his horse's mouth and allowed Prince to graze on the lush grass that grew along the banks of the creek. He then took his rifle and began a short hunt to see what he might find in the way of small game. After just a short walk he came upon a grove of thorn apples. These were exactly like an area he had hunted for ruffed grouse when he was a young lad. He was particularly careful of his movements. He did not have a shotgun and so he knew if he was going to get a bird for dinner he had to catch it sitting on the ground. He slowly sighted through the scope of his rifle and carefully looked under every bush. Finally, his persistence paid off and he saw a grouse fanning his wings on a downed log. He sighted carefully on the bird's head knowing that if he hit the body there would be little left to eat. He took a deep breath and then slowly let it out and squeezed the trigger. The bird completely disappeared and he was afraid that he had missed it, but then realized that if he had the bird would have taken off with the thunderous noise of beating wings.

He made his way to the log and was rewarded by seeing the bird lying still on the other side. He then made his way back to where he had left his horse, mounted, and rode to the edge of the forest to set up camp for the night. There were many dead limbs and branches in the area and he soon had a nice fire going. Having no fry pan or grease he cut the bird into small pieces and used green sticks to hold them above the fire. It would have been nice to have some salt or other seasoning but fortunately, the bird had been eating off of the spicy thorn apples and so had a spicy taste of its own. It was not the best meal that Will had ever had but it was the best meal he had had in this dream.

The following morning he set out and followed the stream in the direction in which it was flowing. He was exceedingly surprised and pleased when he came upon what was a sign of human life, a wagon trail. It was quite wide indicating that the wagons had been traveling two abreast and from the signs, it was well used. He got off his horse for a closer inspection of the tracks and he could see that some of the horses were shod and others were not. He did not know exactly what to make of that fact but he did know that finding the tracks of shod horses indicated intelligent life had passed here.

Another puzzling aspect of the trail was that all the tracks were going in the same direction. He immediately reined his horse in the direction that the wagons were going and set off at a good pace. He could tell by the animal droppings that it had not been a long time since these people had passed by here. He reined his horse in the direction the wagons had gone and hoped that soon he would catch up with them. He had a lot of questions and he hoped they had some answers.

He followed the tracks and noted that they were headed in the general direction that the creek flowed downhill. He reined his horse to the higher ground hoping that he could find some way to cut a few miles off of the journey. When he had gained sufficient altitude he stopped Prince and dismounted. He dropped the lead and allowed the animal to crop some of the tender grass around him. He removed his rifle from the scabbard and began to slowly check out the skyline in all directions. As he glassed the tops of the mountains in the distance he caught a wisp of smoke. He carefully marked the spot in his mind and then continued his scan. He passed around about a quarter of the horizon and then saw another wisp of smoke. And finally, he returned his scope to the direction that the wagons had taken. He hoped that perhaps he could get a glimpse of a cook fire to tell him about how far ahead the wagons might be, but his hopes were not rewarded.

What he did notice was that the wagon trail veered off to the right a few miles ahead. He figured that he could follow around the hillside and cut off perhaps five or ten miles. Of course, that would only work if the trail stayed veering right and did not return to the original direction. He took out a few strips of jerky to munch on as he rode. He returned the rifle to the scabbard, mounted his horse, and set off at a lope. He knew that a man on horseback should be able to make up a lot of ground on horses pulling heavy wagons.

The going was tough as he rode. Many rocks were sticking up and dead trees blocked the trail at various points. He knew he should retreat down the ridge but he wanted as much visual vantage as he could get. Somewhere up ahead were people and he was dying to talk with someone besides his horse. He pushed on well past when the sun gave its best light and heat. He only stopped because he knew that soon it would be too dark to safely ride. Coming upon a spot where a natural spring bubbled up out of the mountainside he dismounted, unsaddled Prince, and began to make camp. He built a good-sized fire not fearing to give away his position. He had seen nothing so far to indicate that anyone in this new world was hostile. He ate a few pieces of jerky and washed it down with water from his canteen. There was fresh grass and water for his horse and so both rider and animal were contented for the night. Before turning in he again scanned the horizon, hoping to catch a glimpse of someone's campfire. And again he was disappointed.

Just before he dozed off, he heard the howling of coyotes. They seemed to be talking to each other from various points of the horizon and a slight chill went up his back. He did not fear coyotes but the song they were singing had a strange lament to it as if they were singing a song of death.

The following morning, before breaking camp he again glassed the horizon. And again in several spots, he noticed small puffs of smoke rising into the air. He thought back to some of the western movies that he had seen throughout his life and he was pretty sure that these were smoke signals. Someone was talking to someone else via the rising plumes. He just wished he knew how to read them.

He decided to angle back down the trail to hopefully make better time. True his present route was shorter, but what he gained in distance he lost in navigating around natural obstacles. He was soon back on the wagon trail having cut several miles off of his journey. And as he rounded a bend he came upon a wagon, but not one being pulled by horses. This wagon lay on its side, clearly the result of having tipped over going a high rate of speed. As Will approached he noticed that arrows were sticking out in several locations on the wrecked wagon and that the horses and people were missing.

He dismounted and made his way to the wagon. It was obvious that the inhabitants had abandoned it in a hurry for most of their belongings were still either inside or scattered around the outside.

Chapter Four - The Battle and the Aftermath

Although there were probably items that he could use, Will figured he needed to hurry on and try to find the other wagons and find out what had happened to this one. Something was not right about this situation. He turned in the direction of the tracks and gently kicked his horse in the side to excite him to a fast pace. He was soon at a full gallop and making up ground rapidly.

After he had traveled what he figured would be a mile at full gallop he reined his horse into a trot. He knew he had to give Prince the chance to cool off but it was then that he heard the gunshots. He was sure that they were coming from the direction he was heading and he cautiously moved in that direction. He had no idea what he might be getting himself into and wanted as much warning as possible. He spied a tall hill off to his left and thought that would give him a good vantage point to survey the situation. He did not want to burn his horse out but he did move Prince up to a lope and reined him towards the crest of the hill.

As he rode he noticed that the gunfire was getting louder and more frequent. Either someone was practicing fast marksmanship or there was a war being waged. He hoped for the former but feared for the later.

When he reached the top of the hill he could see the valley below. Three wagons had formed a triangle and it appeared that about a half dozen mounted riders were charging around the wagons. These riders rode wild-looking horses, much like the wild mustangs that still roam the west. The riders themselves also looked wild with bare chests and backs. Their faces were painted red and white, much like war paint on Indians that he had seen in the movies.

As they rode around the wagons they miraculously hung to the sides of their horses in such a way to be nearly invisible to the people in the wagons and they fired arrows from under their horses' necks. Will marveled at the horsemanship of these riders but he was concerned as to their motivations.

And someone from under the wagons was answering the arrows with rifle fire although it would be difficult for them to hit the riders if that was what they were trying to do.

His first thought was that this was a western movie set and he began looking for the film crew. But for the life of him, he could not figure out where they might be located. Truthfully the vantage point that he had would have been best but there was no filming going on where he was. He tied his horse to the lone tree on the hilltop and pulled his rifle from the scabbard.

"This is not my fight," Will reasoned. "But I am beginning to think that this is a real battle. I may be the only hope those folks in the wagons have."

He sighted through the scope of his rifle and tried to draw a bead on one of the horses. He hated to shoot a horse but he figured if he was making a huge mistake and this was not a battle he would come out better being a horse killer than a murderer. His only problem was that the way the riders were hanging to his side of the horse there was not much room for a bullet to hit the horse without hitting the rider. His first inclination then was to fire a warning shot in front of one of the horses. This he did but with zero results. He then fired a second round even closer but all the spray of dirt did was cause the horse to veer slightly. And then he noticed that when what he believed to be Indians came out the far side of the wagons he had a brief window of opportunity. He figured that he was perhaps 300 yards away from them and he knew his rifle bullet would drop exactly 12 inches at that range.

So he sighted square in the middle of the horse's head and pulled the trigger. For a second he thought he had missed altogether, but then the horse dipped his head and plunged to the ground. The Indian had not expected such a thing to happen and went flying through the air.

Will was afraid that his attempt to save the rider had been for naught and that the Indian may well have broken his neck on impact. But then the fallen rider gained his feet and began to retreat away from the action. Will then aimed at a second horse and again fired. This time the horse pitched to the ground almost immediately and as the rider hit the earth he was left exposed to the rifle fire from under the wagons. He did not get far before they cut him down.

Now the remaining Indians took notice of Will and two of them came charging up the hill towards where he lay prone with his rifle. Will took careful aim at the lead horse and fired. The horse pitched headfirst and the rider flew over his head. Now, Will only had one rider to worry about and he took aim and pulled the trigger only to hear a click. He had lost track of the number of rounds he had fired and the rifle was empty.

Will jumped to his feet and reached for his sidearm. He tugged but the pistol would not come out of the holster. He began to panic and then realized that he had forgotten to remove the hammer strap. As quickly as he could he pushed the pistol back down in the holster and flicked the hammer strap loose. By that time, however, the Indian was almost on top of him and he was in the motion of throwing his long lance. Will drew as quickly as he could and fired one round but not at the warrior. The lance was in full flight when the .357 magnum round hit it squarely on the stone tip and it shattered into several pieces and fell harmlessly to the ground. The Indian seeing this unbelievable marksmanship of his opponent had already swung his horse and was galloping away from danger.

Will returned his attention to the wagon train and saw that all the warriors had disappeared. For the moment the battle appeared to be over. Will reloaded both of his weapons and with his rifle in hand began to lead his horse down the slope toward what he hoped would be civilized people. He was still approximately 100 yards away when someone yelled for him to stop. "That is far enough, stranger. I am not sure which side you are on but there are three rifles trained on your chest. I would not be making any sudden moves."

"Not, too hospitable are you? It seems I just pulled your bacon out of the fire. It did not look like you were doing too well before I decided to back your play."

The voice called back to him. "Really all I saw you do was kill a couple of horses. What kind of damned fool are you? You shoot horses that we could have sold for $20 apiece and you allow savages to live. Their scalps would have brought good money. And where do you think the ones you allowed to escape are going to go?"

"I would imagine that they have had enough fight for a while. They lost three horses and at least one rider today. That should be enough to keep them at bay. Can I come into the wagons? I would like to talk with you about some things."

"Put the rifle back in its scabbard and put the hammer strap back on your side arm and then come in slowly. And don't make any sudden moves. Our trigger fingers are a little itchy at the moment."

Will did as instructed and slowly made his way to the wagons. As he came within a few feet two men and a woman came out of the enclosure. Will looked them over carefully but did his best not to stare. One of the men was approximately six feet two inches tall and weighed well over 200 pounds. The other was a few inches shorter and about 50 pounds lighter. The men were dressed pretty much as you might expect, in cotton shirts and pants but the woman was also dressed in men's clothing. But the rough fabric could not disguise her obvious good looks and fine figure. And there was something vaguely familiar about her as well. Will would have to search his memory later. Right now he needed to find out where he was and how he got here.

"My name is Will Anderson," Will introduced himself. "And you folks would be?"

The large man stepped forward but did not extend his hand. "My name is Frank Parsons and this is my wife Ellen. He then gestured to the second man and said, "And this is my brother Peter."

Will took off his hat and bowed to Ellen and then asked. "I thought from the sounds of the gunfire coming from your wagons that there was more than just the three of you. Do you have wounded that need attention?"

"We lost a man and his wife when we were first attacked a ways back down the trail. And we have a couple of minor wounds being looked at inside the triangle. Now, I would like to know exactly where you came from and how you happened to be out here all by yourself."

"Well, to tell you the truth and I am sure you are not going to believe it, but I don't know how I happened to be here at this time. If I tried to tell you the whole story, you would think I am a crazy person. But I will tell you that I woke up about three days ago in a cave back down the trail a ways. I have no recollection of how I got there or what time period I am in. I have been surviving on a little jerky I had in my saddlebags and whatever game I could collect along the way. I was wondering if I might tag along with you folks until we come to a town. I would be glad to do whatever work might be needed in exchange for my meals."

"Mister, you might be able to sell that snake oil to some folks, but we were not born yesterday. I would feel more comfortable if you just moseyed along. There is an overturned wagon, back down the trail, and if it has not been looted out by now you can find some cooking gear, flour, and coffee. You are welcome to whatever you can scrounge up from there. But if you come within gun range of our wagons, we might just take a shot at you. We do not take kindly to horse shooters in this part of the territory."

"And exactly what territory are we talking about?" asked Will.

"Oh, so we are back to the I don't know where I am nonsense. Ok, I will humor you. We are in the Okala territory. And exactly where do you come from?"

"Well, before I went to sleep and ended up here I was from the State of Ohio."

"I never heard of no place called Ohio. I suggest that you move down the trail. And you might want to keep your eyes alert. Those savages will likely be back and with a whole passel of friends. The next time you meet up, you might want to consider shooting them and taking their horses. Of course, that is if you are alive when it is over." And with that, he gave a deep chuckle and turned back to his wagon.

Chapter Five - The Strange Visitor

Will mounted his horse and turned back down the trail he had ridden here on. He wanted to check out the overturned wagon and see if there was anything he might use to supplement his existence. He carefully scanned the ground in front of him as he rode. He had no idea where the survivors of the attack might be or what their intentions were. Just because most of them were now on foot did not mean that they were not a cause for concern. An arrow fired from a man on foot would be just as deadly as one fired from a man on horseback.

Without incident, he arrived back at the overturned wagon. To make his search easier, he decided to try to turn the wagon back upright. Two of the wheels were broken but he figured that even sitting at an odd angle it would be better than trying to crawl underneath it. So he took his lasso and tied it off to one of the upright supports and hooked it to his saddle horn. He then led Prince away from the wagon until the rope tightened. And then slowly the horse pulled until the wagon tipped back upright. Carefully Will crawled onto the wagon bed and began searching for loose boards that might indicate a hidden compartment. He had been told that the owners of this wagon had been killed in the first attack so anything he found, he could keep.

It took him nearly an hour of hard searching but finally, he found a board that he could lift. Underneath he found a small bag that was wrapped tightly closed with twine. And inside was what he figured was enough gold to keep him in eats for quite some time. Of course, he had no idea where he might be able to spend it in the middle of a territory he had never heard of.

Satisfied that he had found what he was looking for inside the wagon, he climbed down and began to sort out what was usable from what had spilled out when the wagon overturned. He found a frying pan, a coffee pot, a few utensils, and a machete. A bag of flour was still intact and he took that as well. Either the Indians or the other wagons had scavenged most everything else. He wished that they had left some coffee to go with the pot.

It was getting late in the day and Will figured he needed to find someplace less exposed to make camp. He wanted a fire and knew that out in this open prairie it could be seen for miles around. Not too far off the trail, he spied what looked to be a thick stand of willows. If he could find an opening inside of them he might be able to make a small fire that would go undetected by prying eyes. It would be nice to find some small game on the way but after what had happened earlier in the day he was reluctant to fire either of his weapons. There was no sense in drawing any unwanted attention. Perhaps he could make some kind of fried bread out of the flour if he added a little water.

He spent a little time riding along the edge of the willows and after a time came upon a small trail leading to the interior. It was just wide enough for his horse and pushing the willows aside was able to follow it to a small clearing. It was obvious that someone had used this as a camp in the past as there was a pit with blackened wood still in it. He searched the area and found enough dead wood and brush to make a fire. By the time he had his fire started, it was beginning to get dark. He took some of the flour and mixed it with a bit of water from his canteen and made a thick paste. He placed it in the frying pan and held it over the fire. He wished he had a spatula to be able to turn it with but had to be satisfied to scrape some of it onto a knife and flip it that way. It turned out more burned than cooked but as hungry as he was it tasted like a meal fit for a royal family.

He built the fire up again and prepared to spread out his hide and turn in for the night when he heard someone yell out, "Hello the camp. May I come in?"

Will immediately removed the hammer strap from his side arm and then answered. "Who are you and what is your business?"

"I am a friend. I mean you no harm. I would just like to share your fire and have a conversation with you."

"Come on in then, but keep your hands where I can see them. Not everyone in this land is as friendly as I would like."

Very slowly a form emerged out of the growing darkness. He was a tall man, approximately six foot three inches in height, and formidably built. He wore rugged denim clothing and a pistol was strapped to each hip. His shell belt appeared to be full of ammunition and across his chest was a belt that contained what appeared to be shotgun shells although he carried no such weapon in his hands. He did however carry a large closed sack. As he neared the edge of the fire, Will noted that he was deeply tanned as though he had spent a good deal of time in the sun.

The stranger offered his hand and Will accepted it carefully. His handshake was firm and Will could feel the hard calluses that had built up from what must have been hard manual labor.

Will looked the stranger in the eyes and was almost mesmerized. They were deep pools of blackness and they held your attention almost hypnotically. It was difficult for Will to tear himself away from that gaze but with a little shake of his head, he managed to. "What can I do for you this fine evening?" Will asked.

"Well, I was just passing by and smelled your fire. I thought perhaps I might share a cup of coffee and something to eat with you."

"I am afraid, I do not have any coffee and all the food I have is a little fried bread that is not seasoned. But you are welcome to what is left in the pan."

"Perhaps we can do a little better than that." The stranger opened his sack and produced a small pouch that proved to contain some ground coffee. He also produced a small metal grate much as you might find on a small grill and placed it over the fire. He extracted a coffee pot and went about the chore of adding water and coffee and set it on the grate over the fire.

While the coffee was cooking, Will took the opportunity to introduce himself. He found out that the stranger's name was Jack although no last name was offered.

"Well, Jack, exactly how did you happen upon my camp? I thought I was pretty well concealed inside this stand of willows."

"As I mentioned I smelled your fire although I will admit that I have had my eyes on you for a couple of days. You have not exactly been invisible riding out in the open and staying mostly on the high ridges. I imagine that others have taken notice of your presence as well, especially after the show you put on today."

"And just what do you know about what happened today?" Will inquired.

"Try to follow along here, Will. I already told you that I had been keeping my eyes on you for a couple of days. That would imply that I might have witnessed your great horse killing spree, now would it not?"

Will's hackles started to rise at what he perceived to be the stranger's belligerence. "Yes, you told me but you haven't told me why. Nor did I understand that meant 24 hours a day. So why don't you clue me in? Why are you watching me and you might also impart a little information on where I am and how I got to be here?"

"Wow, for an intelligent man you are a little slow on the uptake. You got here because you wished it so. And it doesn't matter where you are or what point in time you are. You simply exist at this moment."

"Ok, now you have completely lost me. Are you saying that I am in some kind of an alternate reality?"

"Again let me emphasize to you that where you are is not the important element. What you are is much more important. And from what I witnessed today, I have my doubts about what you are."

"You keep talking in riddles. Why not just come out and tell me what I did today that causes you concern? I will admit that I was unsure about getting involved in that battle. It is not always easy to tell which side is which. But all I had to go on was what I had learned from history. Not that the Indians were always to blame mind you, but it appeared in this instance that they were the aggressors. I tried to stop them with as little loss of human life as was possible."

"Let me get this straight?" Jack inquired. "You did not know which side was which and so you chose to kill innocent animals in deference to killing humans that may or may not have been innocent. If I remember right you hold God to a much higher standard than that."

"Oh, so now I am beginning to understand. So are you a messenger of God, sent here to teach me a lesson? If so you are way out of your league. What happened today was that I did not have all the information to make an intelligent decision. God is supposed to be all-knowing and all-seeing. He knows who is right and who is wrong, so it should be easy for him to make the right decision in every instance."

"So you are assuming that there always is a right side and a wrong side, is that it? Tell me who was the right side in today's skirmish? Surely the horses were not on the wrong side."

"So let me ask you since you were there and are somehow connected to the great and almighty being, why did you not step in? You surely knew who was at fault."

"First let me answer you by saying, it was not my fight. But you waded right in as if you knew all the particulars. And now later when you are questioned you use the excuse that you did not know what you were doing. Would you allow God that same excuse?"

"Of course not," Will replied. "I have already told you that God is supposed to know everything. Why did he not intervene?"

"And if he had, what would you have learned from that? Would you have all of a sudden got down on your knees and given praise to him? Or would you have found some other reason to find fault? I will let you think about that as we eat and have a cup of coffee."

Will was amazed. He had not realized that any food was being cooked, but when he turned around the stranger was handing him a big plate of beans that smelled delicious and a cup of strong hot coffee. As Will ate what was the best meal he had enjoyed since waking up in the cave he thought about all the things the stranger had told him. It bothered him that perhaps he had chosen to do something that was totally against logical thinking. He too regretted killing those horses but he still could not reconcile how killing humans would have been better. And then he realized that at least indirectly he had been responsible for the death of at least one human as well. If he had not shot the horse out from under one rider, he would not have been exposed to the rifle fire coming from the wagons.

Will looked up to continue his conversation with Jack only to realize that Jack was no longer there. The coffee pot still sat on the grill but both his and Jack's plates were missing, as was whatever utensil had been used to cook the beans. Will waited for what he perceived to be an hour, and called out several times for Jack but when he received no answer he curled up under his animal skin and drifted off to an uneasy sleep. That night he had terrible dreams of dead snakes and dead horses. He tossed and turned and had a great deal of difficulty keeping himself under the warm skin. And when he awoke he was cold and his body felt like it had been through a grinder.

There were only a few live coals and so he simply covered them up with dirt and saddled his mount. He could hear running water close by and so he led Prince in that direction. Soon he came upon a fast-moving stream and he allowed his horse to drink his fill before starting their day's journey. He had no idea where he was going but he figured that he could tag along behind the wagon train if he was careful and stayed out of sight. Unlike him, they surely must know where there was civilization.

As he emerged from the willows and started to climb up to the wagon trail he smelled what he was sure was the brewing of coffee. And just around the first bend, he came upon Jack sitting on a large rock with a cup in his hand.

Chapter Six - A Traveling Companion

Jack looked up at him and gestured for him to get down and join him. When Will obeyed Jack handed him a cup of steaming coffee. As he took a sip, Jack asked. "It looks like you had a rough night, was there something keeping you awake?"

"You seem to be quite perceptive," said Will. "But then I imagine you put some of those thoughts in my dreams. Still teaching me lessons are you?"

Jack patted the rock beside him. "Here have a seat and drink your coffee. And if you like I even have a plate of eggs and some trail bread you might like."

"Just where did you get eggs out here in the middle of nowhere?"

"Oh, you can get about anything you want if you know where to look. Everything that a man needs to live has been provided for him. You just have to put in the effort to learn what surrounds you."

"Yes, I have noticed. So far I have found a couple of blackberry patches a couple of lone apple trees and a partridge. I am just living high off the hog. And by the way, I notice that so far you have not produced any meat to eat. Is there a rule against eating the flesh of animals? It seems I remember in the Bible that most animals could be harvested for food."

"Well, if you want to be precise about it, not most animals." Replied Jack. "Only those that clove the hoof and chew the cud but that was a different time and a different place. Those animals such as cows and sheep were less susceptible to disease than others. There is no firm rule as to what you can take to eat. I just choose not to kill anything if I do not have to."

"I notice that you are pretty well-armed for someone that chooses not to kill. Why the two gun rig and obviously somewhere a shotgun?"

"Oh, they are for show mostly. People expect to see someone armed to the teeth in this place. If I did not appear that I could protect myself, I might have to prove myself more often. You may remember yesterday when you shot that spear out of the air, your antagonist took off quickly. It is kind of like that."

Will took the plate of eggs that were offered, noticing that they were small but plentiful. He soaked up some of the yolks with the strange bread and marveled at how good they tasted. "You sure know how to cook. Those beans last night and now these eggs and bread. I doubt that a French chef could do much better."

"It may have something to do with the fact that you have nearly starved for the last couple of days. And of course, all this fresh air gives a man a good appetite. I see that you are nearly done, so let's take the plates over to that spring by the rock and rinse them off."

Again Will was surprised. He had been sitting here conversing with Jack and had not noticed that the spring even existed. Surely he was not that unaware of his surroundings. He began to suspect that Jack might have supernatural powers. As Will rinsed off the plates and the coffee pot, Jack disappeared from view for a few minutes. When he returned he was leading a large black horse with wild eyes and prancing feet. There was not a spot visible on the horse that was not shining black including the tip of his nose.

"Wow, that is one powerful-looking horse you have there. What do you call him?"

"You mean like an assigned name. I have never gotten around to it. I know who he is and he seems to know me and it isn't that we talk very often. I guess I could call him king. But that might make your horse jealous since you have assigned him to a lower rank. Come on, we can ponder the idea as we ride."

Soon the gear was washed and stowed and the men were mounted. Will felt a little small riding beside the huge monster of a horse but Jack did not seem to notice the difference or if he did he did not remark on it. Jack turned up the trail heading in the direction that the wagons had traveled the day before. He seemed to know without being told where Will wanted to go.

As they passed by the spot where the battle had taken place the day before, Will turned to Jack and asked him where they were going. "Why wherever you want to go."

"How about Disneyland then?" Will remarked. "How long do you think it will take us to get there?"

"Perhaps another lifetime," was Jacks' answer. "For now, let's take a little shortcut up through this gap to our right. I have a feeling that Ellen is going to need some assistance shortly and perhaps we can get to her quicker this way." And with that, he swung his big horse off the trail and headed towards a gap in the mountains to his right.

Will was now exceedingly curious about his traveling companion. How did he know who Ellen was if he was only watching Will as he stated the previous evening? And how could he know what was going to take place in the future? He knew he could just ask the man but most of what Jack had told him came in the form of riddles.

As they topped the first rise Will could see across miles of open expanse. Somewhere in the distance, he could see a dark column of smoke rising above the lush green of the land below him. Instinctively he knew that smoke did not bode well for Ellen. He immediately put his heels to his horse's side urging the loyal animal to full speed. But something told him that no matter how fast he went he was going to be too late. He made a quick check to his right to see if Jack was still with him but he saw nothing of the huge black horse or of the mysterious man that rode him. "Well, I guess I will have to take care of this myself." He thought.

He allowed his horse to stretch out for several minutes and then began to rein him in. It would do no one any good if he ran his horse to death. And besides, he had no idea of what lay ahead of him. Running blindly into a situation would not be a prudent thing to do. The land was rolling and as he topped another rise he could now see the cause of the smoke. A wagon was burning and another was stopped just up the line. Bare-breasted men who were doing everything possible to subdue someone that was putting up more fight than they expected surrounded that wagon. Not having time to think of a better option, Will removed the hammer strap from his sidearm and again urged his mount forward and into the fray.

He was not sure how many of the enemies were present but he did not have the choice to wait to find out. As soon as he was near enough to be within pistol range he snapped off a shot at a rider and was rewarded as the man pitched forward and fell to the ground. Two others saw a new threat and turned their war ponies towards him leaving the person they had been trying to subdue. Will leaned down as an arrow sailed towards him and fired another shot. Again a horse ran free without a rider. Will turned his attention to the second rider and again fired. He had not wanted to kill anyone but there was no choice and a third rider fell. He charged onward directly towards the stopped wagon. He saw that there were no horses attached and so he knew that if anyone were still alive they would have no means of escape. Several painted ponies stood without riders and Will knew at least four more Indians were waiting to oppose him. Unfortunately, he only had three more shots in his six-shooter.

At full gallop, Will charged around the front of the wagon only to see three braves holding down a nearly naked woman and a fourth preparing to mount her. Again and again and again Will's pistol roared and now only one brave stood against him. He did not have time to reload or to pull his rifle from its scabbard. The brave had left the woman and had picked up his bow and was notching an arrow onto the string when Will's horse hit him solidly and sent him spinning to the ground. Will quickly dismounted, ejected the spent brass from his pistol, and reloaded fresh cartridges. But now there did not seem to be anyone left in opposition to him. He first checked the fallen warrior not wanting to leave a threat to his rear. But the man was no longer a threat. A thousand pounds of horse had made sure of that. He quickly but cautiously approached the woman on the ground, keeping a close eye out for any hostiles that may have been lurking nearby.

He could see that the woman before him was the one who had been introduced to him as Ellen. She had put up quite a fight it appeared, as her knuckles were bloody. But she had paid a price as well. Her face looked as if a mule had kicked it and both her arms and legs were bruised and cut. And she was unconscious. Will did not know what to do. He had no medical training but he did know that he should cover her up. He made his way to the wagon and opened the back in search of a blanket. He found what he was looking for but he also found Ellen's husband. The entire top of his head was missing and several arrows protruded from his body. Will figured when he had a chance to inspect the burning wagon he would find a similar fate had befallen the occupants.

He took the blanket back to the fallen woman and covered her as best he could. He took one of his canteens from off his saddle and withdrew a clean kerchief from his pack. He wet the cloth and daubed gently against the woman's face trying to remove as much dried blood as possible to see how extensive her wounds were. "Dear God, what I wouldn't give for a doctor, right now." He wished. And as if in answer to a prayer he saw a large black horse coming towards him. And following behind was the missing team.

Jack rode up close to them and dismounted. He quickly pulled a sack from the back of his saddle and squatted down next to Ellen.

"Will, start a fire and get some water boiling. She has a lot of nasty cuts that will need to be cleaned. I will do my best to help her while you are gone. I doubt that there are any more of what you call Indians around but keep your eyes peeled just in case. By the time Will had gotten a fire going and water on to boil, Jack had most of Ellen's injuries attended to. He had propped his saddlebags under her head and had again covered her with a blanket.

"I have done what I could for her. Now we just need to wait and see if she wakes up. If you had been much later getting to her I am afraid she would not have survived. Normally they would have taken her for a slave but she put up such a fierce fight that they were so angry they just wanted to use and then kill her."

"And exactly where were you when I was facing seven hostile Indians by myself?" Will demanded.

"Again, Will this was not my fight. I will do what I can to be of assistance to you. But killing is not part of my job description."

"But standing by and watching people die is?" Will asked. "Did you ever consider that if you had backed me up maybe I would not have had to kill these people?"

"Everyone has free will, Will. You could have chosen to ignore what was happening here and just rode on. If you had seven people would be alive that are now dead and one person that is now alive would have been dead. You will have to decide if you did the right thing or not."

"So we are back to the free will thing again. I suppose all the Jews that were sent to Hitler's gas chambers had free will. I suppose Ellen had free will when three strong men were holding her down so that a fourth could rape her."

Jack looked directly into Will's eyes. "I guess you think I know what you are talking about when you mention Jews or Hitler. And as for Ellen, she had free will when she decided to invade the Indian's land. She and her husband could have stayed where they were and lived their lives in relative comfort but they chose instead to move into hostile territory. They both understood that there were risks involved. That is free will, Will."

"It seems to me that free will usually works out best for those with evil intentions." Will shot back.

"And you are the one to decide who is evil and who is righteous? Would you like to take a look at the families that are grieving tonight because you decided you would intervene in what was none of your business?"

Will was taken aback by the vehemence in Jack's voice. Until now all of their confrontations had been low-key. But now it seemed Jack was taking the battle to him and he did not understand why.

"I doubt that we will settle anything tonight." Stated Jack. "Let's have a little something to eat and a cup of coffee. Perhaps Ellen will be awake in the morning and we will be able to move out. There is a small town about 30 miles from here that has a doctor. I would like to get her looked at as soon as possible. And then as if from nowhere Jack produced a plate of beans and a steaming hot cup of coffee."

Once the food was eaten and the coffee drunk, Jack told Will to get some sleep. That he would stand the first watch.

As Will drifted off to a troubled sleep all he could see behind his closed eyes was the shocked look of that brave as Prince collided with his body.

Will woke to the smell of coffee brewing and eggs frying. He really wished he knew the secret of magically appearing eggs but he knew that asking Jack would only result in riddles. He also noted that the sun was fairly high in the sky. "Why didn't you wake me for the second watch?" Will asked.

"Oh, I don't need a lot of sleep. And I figured you would need all the strength you could get before today was over. I was hoping to be started on the trail today but Ellen is still unconscious and I don't feel good about jostling her over the trail until she can tell us more about her injuries. After breakfast, I guess we should go inspect the other wagon. I imagine there are more dead to bury."

"You imagine, are you not all-knowing?"

"Will you have me confused with someone with much greater powers than I possess. My powers are limited to observation. And right now I observe that you are confused."

After checking on Ellen's condition one more time, Will and Jack mounted their horses and made their way back to the burned-out wagon. It was pretty much as Will had thought. Two men and a woman lay with their bodies riddled with arrows and their scalps removed. It appeared that the woman had not been raped, as her clothing was still intact. Perhaps she had been killed from a distance when the attack began saving her from a greater indignity.

The two men made a travois from some wood that had survived the fire and a couple of blankets that had been thrown free during the attack. They positioned the bodies onto the crude means of transportation and secured them behind Prince and began a slow retreat to the wagon where Ellen lay unconscious.

Will searched through the wagon and found a couple of shovels. Handing one to Jack he said. "Looks like we have a lot of digging to do. I certainly hope that this is not rocky ground."

"It might be easier if we just put the bodies all in one pile and burned them. It seems a waste of time and effort to dig 11 holes and then fill them in again."

"I do not understand you. I thought you would have more respect for the dead."

"I didn't mean to get your shorts all balled up in a knot. Give me the shovel and let's get this over with."

It took the better part of the day to dig the graves and then roll the bodies into them. They had no way of marking which graves were which but Will made certain to put Ellen's husband in the one closest to the wagon. He was sure that she would want to pay her respects once she awoke. When they were ready to be recovered Will turned to Jack and asked. "Should we say something before we fill in the graves?"

"If it makes you feel better, be my guest. It will not matter one way or another to these eleven departed people."

Having no idea what might be said on this solemn occasion, Will just grabbed his shovel and began filling in the holes. "At least, he thought, they are where animals will not be feasting on them."

Ellen awoke later that day and Jack helped her to sit up. She did not seem to know where she was or how she had gotten here for a brief time. But Jack had prepared a weak broth and helped her to eat a little bit of it. She finally regained a little recognition and turned to see Will sitting across from where she was propped up. "Well, if it isn't the great horse killer. I thought my husband warned you not to come close to our wagons again?" She then began to seriously study her surroundings. "She wrinkled her brow as if she was trying to remember something and then began to get quite animated. "Where is Frank? Please, God, don't tell me those savages got him."

Jack merely put his arms around her shoulders and drew her to him. He gently rocked her back and forth as tears of understanding overtook her and horrible sobs shook her body. No one had to tell her what had happened as the memory of the attack rolled over her and broke her spirit into a hundred pieces.

When she had finally cried all the tears that she had in her body, she regained control and forced herself to look at Will. "This is all your fault you know. If you had killed those savages when you had the chance this would never have happened. Frank and our friends would still be alive. Now I have no idea what I am going to do."

Not knowing what to say in his defense, Will merely kept quiet. Jack, however, did speak up. "Ellen, I know that you have suffered a great loss. The first thing we need to do is to get you to a doctor. You suffered a lot of trauma, much more than I can treat. There is a town about 30 miles from here. If we make good time we can be there in about three days."

"I am not going anywhere without my husband. I am not going to leave him all alone out here in the middle of nowhere."

"I am truly sorry, but I am afraid you have no choice. We buried Frank not too far from where your wagon is sitting. There would be no point in digging up the grave now just to have him decompose on the trail. Now, try to relax. We leave at first light."

Chapter Seven - Outlaws on the Trail

The morning broke with a cold wind blowing across the plains. Although, no rain was falling it was obvious from the cloud formations that some type of storm was moving in. Even the horses seemed to be nervous about what might be coming. Wanting to make as much headway as possible before they might be forced to once again make camp, they only had a cup of hot coffee and some dried fruit that Ellen had in her wagon. She was adamant that she was not going to leave her dead husband all alone in an unmarked grave beside the wagon tracks so Jack had to force her up onto the wagon seat. He then tied his horse on behind the wagon and climbed up next to the bereaved widow and urged the team onward.

Will mounted his horse and took the point keeping a close eye out for trouble of any kind. As he rode he checked the loads in his pistol and rifle to make sure both were ready for whatever might come his way. His mind drifted back to the conversation he had with Jack and how upset the big man seemed to be with him. True this might not have been his fight but when presented with the alternative he could not see that he had a huge amount of choice in the matter. One lone woman being ravished by seven mighty men did not seem like a fair fight. And Will prided himself on being fair.

The first drops of rain came big and plump spraying dust where they fell. Within minutes the rain was so thick that the men had difficulty making out the wagon tracks ahead of them.

"We need to find shelter." Yelled Jack. "I don't like the looks of those clouds off in the distance."

Will strained his eyes but for the life of him, he could not see what Jack was looking at. How could the man see anything off in the distance when Will could not see 10 feet in front of his face? "I don't know how you can see any clouds. This rain is so thick that I can barely see the front end of my horse."

"Stay close to the wagon. I will lead the way. Apparently, my eyesight is a little better than yours." Jack yelled above the roar of the storm. He urged the team to move more quickly and he soon pulled up against a large rock outcropping that seemed to block the wind. By that time both humans and animals were completely soaked. But now most of the rain flew over their heads. All three humans climbed into the back of the wagon. Within minutes they had all three shed their wet clothes and wrapped themselves in blankets that they found. Even Ellen had not hesitated to take off her wet clothes with two strange men present. It was as if she knew that the greater danger was pneumonia over anything these two might try.

And then as if it had never happened the rain and wind stopped. The sun came out and the air began to immediately dry. It was like someone had turned the spigot and turned off the hose. Will immediately went to check on the welfare of the animals. Hopefully, they were better adapted to deal with such a downpour than humans were. Three of the horses, the team, and Jack's behemoth were fastened to the wagon and so they stood where they had been left. Prince, however, had moved away from the wagon and was nowhere to be seen. Will started to panic hoping that the loyal horse had not been carried away by the high winds that had accompanied the rain. He called several times and then set off on foot. He hoped to be able to find tracks that he could follow but was soon disappointed as the ferocity of the storm had even wiped out the wagon trail.

After searching for what seemed to be a long time, Will finally went back to the wagon. He told Jack that his horse had disappeared and that he would need to drive the wagon while Jack rode his horse.

Jack readily agreed and told Will that he was more comfortable on horseback than on a wagon seat anyway. And then he looked at Ellen's face and knew that Will was not going to be comfortable with the new arrangement.

As they set off trying as best they could to pick a trail across the plains Will looked to Ellen and tried to tell her how sorry he was that this had happened to her. He asked her what she planned to do, but received no answer. It was obvious that Ellen still held him responsible for the death of her husband.

"I hope someday you will understand what a difficult position I was in that first day we met. At first, I thought what I was seeing was a movie set and not a real-life attack on your wagon train. I kept looking around for the camera crew but I could not find them. And even when I shot the first horse I was still not sure that it was real. By the time I had convinced myself of what was going on, the battle was over and the Indians had already fled. You have to understand I am not a killer."

Ellen just looked at him as if he had two heads and was part of a carnival routine. "I have no idea what you are talking about. What is a movie set and what is a camera crew? And I guess you are calling the savages that attacked us Indians. I am not sure where you got that term. They are Montross warriors and their sole purpose in life is to kill anyone that comes to what they perceive as their land."

"If you knew the danger then why did you come this way?" Will asked her.

"We started out with a much larger wagon train. We felt we were strong enough to repel any attack that might be thrown at us. But a few days ago the rest of the wagons changed their minds and decided to go a different way. Frank and I had purchased some land not too far from here. We had used all of our life savings for that land and we just could not abandon our dreams. So two other families and I decided to forge on alone. That first attack took us completely by surprise and we lost one of the wagons and two of the settlers. Even so, if you had not shown up and interfered we would have likely killed all the attackers and we would have made the rest of the trip uneventfully. But because of you, I have lost everything."

"Why do you say you have lost everything? I know it will be harder but you still own the land and I will help you get to it."

"You really are clueless aren't you? Women cannot own land. Without my husband, I will be forced to cede the land to the territorial government. And then I will be sent to a camp for single women. Those camps are nothing but slave labor camps. Unless one of the guards decides to take me as his personal servant I will spend the rest of my life working for others. So you see you really did me no favors by saving my life back there. It would have been a kindness to have let the savages kill me."

Will could not believe what he was hearing. Had he been sent to a time when women were treated as slaves simply because they did not have a husband as a protector? And why was it that every decision he made was the wrong one? Surely that could not be a coincidence. Maybe Jack would be able to cast more light on the situation when they stopped for the night.

The going became more and more difficult as they were constantly having to go around huge mud holes and downed trees. What had once been a passable trail had been reduced to a difficult obstacle course. And finally, Jack rode up beside the wagon and made an announcement. "We are not going to be able to continue on our present course. The streams ahead are now overflowing their banks and while the horses might be able to traverse them the wagon would never make it. I seem to remember that there is another way we could take and it would even be a little shorter."

"That sounds good. Why did we not go that way, to begin with?"

"Rumor has it that there are desperados that control the passage between the mountains. If we had another choice I would rather take it."

"Well, if what Ellen tells me is true, we might just as well abandon the wagon anyway. She is not going to be allowed to keep her belongings once we get to the next town in any event. Wouldn't we be better off letting her ride one of the team and avoid going through that treacherous stretch of road?"

"I would leave that decision to Ellen," Jack stated. "However, she would be giving up her only hope of remaining autonomous."

"I am confused. She told me that women could not own property and that she would be assigned to a work camp because she had no husband."

"But what she did not tell you is that there are some men that would take her as their wife just because she has something of value. Rather than giving up her wagon and belongings, she could trade them for the comfort of sharing a home with someone new."

"What a barbaric world you sent me to. I too would have been happier if when I closed my eyes I could have been allowed nothingness. But I guess someone thought I needed to be taught a lesson and sent me here."

"First understand. I did not send you anywhere. Your argumentative attitude was the reason you ended up here. You knew so much more than your creator so this was a little test to see how you would fare when forced to make difficult decisions. How would you say you have scored so far?"

"I am not sure that any of this has been a fair test." Will shot back. "I think that no matter what course of action I had taken it would have been turned around to be wrong. I think your creator as you call him, enjoys setting his subjects up to fail. Why don't you just turn off the holographic imager?

And then for the first time, Jack allowed his guard to fall just a little bit. "This isn't an episode of "Star Trek," he said. "Everything you see and hear is real."

"Maybe so," Will replied. "But it seems a lot like an episode of "The Twilight Zone".

Having heard enough of the two men's drivel, Ellen interrupted. "I have no idea what the two of you are talking about but while you are making allusions to things I have never heard of we are sitting in the middle of a wagon track with nightfall rapidly approaching. Don't you think we should be trying to find a good spot to make camp?"

Jack raised his hand and gestured for us to follow him much like a Captain of the cavalry or an old wagon master would. He led us off what used to be the beaten path and along a hard rock trail that was barely wide enough for the team and wagon. The trail led upward towards some distant peaks. Will could see no way that this rugged path could lead them where they were going quicker than sticking to the level ground but he just concentrated on keeping the wagon on the trail.

They had steadily climbed for a couple of hours and the light of day was beginning to fade when Jack raised his hand in a gesture for the wagon to halt. He had chosen a somewhat level patch of ground with another miracle spring of water on one side. There were also a few adult trees growing nearby and enough dead limbs had dropped off of them to supply plenty of firewood. While Will went to gather firewood Jack mounted his horse and went on a scouting mission. He was gone until after dark and by the time he returned Ellen had fixed a meal using items she had brought with her. There were trail biscuits, fried bacon, and canned fruit for dessert. And to top it off some strong coffee.

Will heard the riders coming and instinctively took the hammer strap off of his sidearm. He eased it out of his holster and held it at his side just in case something unfriendly appeared. He expected Jack at any time but he was positive that more than one horse was approaching and so he wanted to be ready for anything. But then Jack materialized out of the darkness and to Will's happy amazement he was leading another horse behind his. And Will was elated to see that the horse was Prince.

"I found him contentedly chewing on some lush grass just over the rise. I am sure he will be happy when you remove his saddle and brush him down. I imagine he wandered off during the storm and then did not know how to get back. He has probably been looking for you ever since."

Will immediately removed the saddle from the horse and checked him over as best he could in the dim light of the fire. He saw no signs of saddle sores or other injuries and since he did not speak horse he could not ask Prince if he was injured. Satisfied that there was little else he could do he secured a rope around his horse's neck and tied it to a downed log. He wanted to make sure that the horse was still there in the morning. He then pulled his rifle from the scabbard and took it back to the fire. He pulled a small tin of grease from his saddlebags and went through the process of making sure the weapon was clean dry and lubricated. He was thankful that he had not needed a long gun in the past, but he did not want to face many more days in this troubled land without one.

The following day passed without incident. They made good headway even with the trail being slightly uphill. By the time they made camp that night, they were fairly close to the gap between the mountains that Jack had warned might be controlled by highwaymen. Jack again asked if they wanted to leave the wagon and skirt the dangerous passage but Ellen would have none of that.

"If you two want to go around, you have my blessing. I will drive the team straight through that gap and anyone that tries to stop me will have to face my rifle."

When morning came Will was not overly surprised to find that Jack had left camp. He carefully checked his weapons to make sure they were in good order and loaded to the max. "I think we are on our own today. Jack always seems to know when there is going to be a fight and he carefully avoids it. Make sure your rifle is loaded and ready. I am almost positive we will be facing tough opposition today."

They drove out with Will in the lead on Prince. The closer they got to the opening between the mountains, the more the hair was standing up on the back of his neck. He carefully scanned the area with his riflescope and was sure he saw light reflecting off of metal about a half-mile ahead. He walked his horse back to the wagon and informed Ellen that they may soon have to make a fight of it. He instructed her that if trouble reared its ugly head she was to put the whip to the team and let him worry about holding the bandits at bay. Just as they reached the spot where the two mountains almost came together a rider appeared from behind a large boulder. He had a rifle in his hand and raised the other as a sign that the man and woman should come to a halt.

"Senor that is a nice gun you have there on your hip. And that is also a nice-looking horse you are riding. I think I might like to have a horse and a gun like that. How much do you want for them?"

"Neither one is for sale so if you don't mind move your horse off the trail and allow us to proceed."

"I don't think so, senor. You see to pass through this territory you have to pay a toll. And the toll that I have set for today is three horses, two rifles, one pistol, one wagon, and one woman. If you pay the toll you can walk away with your life. If not, well my friends and I will have to kill you and take the toll anyway." And with that, he waved his hand in the air and three other riders came out from behind rocks to join him. "I know that you now realize that you do not have a choice so please unbuckle your gun belt and let it fall to the ground, then get down from your horse and start walking away."

"I am a little surprised." Will began. "Have you not heard of my reputation? Perhaps you would like to save yourself some trouble by allowing us to pass."

"I have heard of you senor. You are the mighty horse killer. Of course, if you kill my horse, I will still have yours to ride, no? And if you have not noticed I already have my gun out. I think you stand no chance in this fight."

"You know, I once saw a television show called "The Arizona Rangers". It seems there was an actor on that show that was the fast-draw champion of the world. They said that he could draw and fire in less than three-tenths of a second. And they also said it took the eye 3 tenths of a second to recognize movement and transfer that knowledge to the brain. So a man could theoretically be dead before his eye told his brain to pull a trigger. Now I don't claim to be that fast but I know I am faster than a rattlesnake. If you do not drop your rifle and clear the trail we will find out how fast I am."

"Perhaps you are fast with a gun, but surely you don't think you are fast enough to take all four of us before we get you?"

"I don't know if I can take all four of you or not, but I am positive I can take you." Like lightning Will's hand swept down to his gun. Before the big man could even react the bullet slammed into his chest and he slumped from his saddle. Will yelled for Ellen to give her horses the whip and the wagon surged forward just as the other three outlaws reached for their guns. Will fired again and another outlaw bit the dust. The remaining two tried desperately to get their guns aligned but bullets also took them down. Ellen had just cleared the gap between the mountains when out of the corner of Will's eye he saw a man rise from behind a rock with a rifle in his hand. He was taking dead aim at Ellen but unfortunately, he was out of pistol range. Will could do nothing but watch, as he did not have the time to pull his rifle and sight on the man. But something unexpected happened. A man on a large black horse appeared near the man with the rifle. His pistols were spitting fire and bullets were bouncing all around the lone bandit. Without hesitation, the bandit dropped his rifle and raised his hands.

Will reloaded his pistol and slowly rode towards the speeding wagon and the lone rider on the black horse. "Well, Jack I am surprised to see you but I am very grateful. What happened to this is not my fight?"

"I saw no harm in helping out a fellow human as long as I did not have to kill anyone to do it. I am kind of surprised to see that you came through another scrape without even a nick. I hear those boys were real bad hombres. I don't suppose you want to take the time to gather up their bodies and take them to town. It is possible they have rewards for their capture and probably dead or alive."

"How far is it to this town you talked about?"

"We can be there in a couple of hours, I would think."

"Then let's see if we can catch Ellen. We can load the bodies up in the wagon and take them to town. It should be easier than digging four more graves."

Chapter Eight - The Town of Whipple

It was just getting dusk as they pulled into the little town. It was actually more like a spot in the road than a town. There were maybe half a dozen buildings on Main Street, the only street in fact. There was a saloon, a mercantile, a livery stable a hotel, and a Sheriff's office. They pulled up in front of the law keepers place and Jack dismounted from his horse and went inside. He was gone for more than a few minutes when he came out with a large rotund man with a star pinned to his chest. They quickly walked around to the back of the wagon and threw the flap aside. The Sheriff examined each body and then turned to Jack. "Yes, these are all wanted men with a reward on their heads. I will have to check my posters but I imagine the total will come to around $500. If you take them down to the undertakers, he will take them off your hands. It will take a few days to get the money delivered here. I am sure you will not want to wait around for it so if you let me know where you are headed I can have it forwarded to you.

Jack replied. "I don't think that any of us are in a hurry to hit the trail. It has been a trying trip and a little downtime might be good for us."

The Sheriff looked disappointed and then said. "To be honest with you I would just as soon that you moved along. Folks don't take too kindly to bounty hunters in these parts and then there is always the possibility that some of these boy's friends may come looking for revenge."

Will finally decided to weigh in on the issue. "Isn't that your job Sheriff? Keeping the peace I mean. And we are not bounty hunters. We were just traveling on the road when these men tried to rob and murder us. If I had been a touch slower on the draw we would be lying dead beside the trail."

"You made that sound like you were the only one involved in the gunplay. Surely you are not going to tell me that you killed all four of these outlaws by yourself." The Sheriff stated with an incredulous look on his face. "And there is another matter we need to discuss before you leave. It involves the woman in the wagon. Are you her husband?"

"I am not. Is that important?"

"Single women are not allowed to stay within the town limits unless under a male relative's supervision."

"And who made up an asinine rule like that?" Will asked.

"It doesn't matter who made up the rule. It only matters that I am obliged to enforce it. Unless she has a sponsor I will have to take her into custody and turn her over to the magistrate in the morning for processing."

Will casually removed the hammer strap from his pistol. Swinging his mount to directly face the Sheriff he looked him straight in the eye. "I would not try taking her into custody if I was you. I don't want any trouble with the law but I feel kind of responsible for this lady. And I am not going to stand by and allow her to be abused without making an account of myself."

The Sheriff moved his hand closer to the butt of his revolver but the look in Will's eyes deterred him from trying to draw the weapon. Drop your dead off down the street and clear out of town. You may be faster than I am but I can have a dozen deputies here in a couple of hours. If you are still within my jurisdiction I will have no choice but to arrest you. The law is the law."

"Just how far out of town does your jurisdiction go?" Jack broke in.

"About 20 miles but if you are out of my immediate sight I might not have cause to look for you. But mark my words you do not want to spend a lot of time camping nearby."

"We will be on our way Sheriff. I will send word where you can forward the money for the bounties." Jack replied.

It was fully dark by the time the three travelers cleared the town limits. They found a place just off the trail with ready water and grass for the horses and made camp. Once again they dined on canned goods and camp bread and Will hoped that sometime in the near future he would get a chance to have a real sit-down meal at a real dining establishment. Once the horses were taken care of and they had eaten their meager fare and Ellen had retired to the wagon for the night, Will turned to Jack and asked. "What are we going to do about Ellen? Surely there must be something that can be done to allow her to take possession of the land she legally purchased."

"I have been thinking about that. It would be easier if she had a male relative that could sponsor her. But the closest relatives she has are way back East. She does not think that any of them would give up the easy life and come out here just to help her out."

"Well, there must be something that can be done. It certainly is not fair that a woman has to give up everything she owns just because of her gender."

"Why don't you marry her and settle down on her land?" Jack asked with a grin.

"I doubt that she would welcome me as her husband. Surely there must be some way around this barbaric practice of treating women as property."

"Men learned something from your age. They learned that they had reason to fear strong single women. Some of that might date back to your Biblical teachings. From the very beginning, men fell victim to their women's wiles. I think you refer to it as the account of The Garden Of Eden. Eve tempted Adam with an apple and he lost eternal life."

"That is as good a reason as any for men to become women owners I guess." Will retorted. "Of course, there is nothing to suggest that Eve held a gun to Adam's head and made him chew."

"Haven't you ever done something for a woman just because you wanted to please her?"

"Of course, I have. And I have done things for men because I wanted to please them, but I don't blame any of them for my decisions."

"So Ellen had nothing to do with the fact that you killed 11 men?"

"So what is your point? Was I brought here so that you could convince me that women are evil and that I should join the enslave-all-women society?"

"My point is that you are still making assumptions based on nothing more than your own ideas. According to you the only person that knows what is best is Will Anderson."

"You haven't shown me anything convincing enough to alter that viewpoint. Since this whole dream sequence of yours is clearly a waste of time, perhaps you should just put me back in the cave and let me go back to sleep."

"Nothing is stopping you from returning to that location if you can find it. If you do you are welcome to close your eyes and go to sleep. But of course, you will have to open them again the next morning and decide what you want to do with that day of your life, much the same as you will have to decide what to do tomorrow when you wake up.

Chapter Nine - Salem All Over Again

When Will opened his eyes the next day he did so with a feeling that something drastic had changed. He was used to waking up to the smell of breakfast cooking and coffee brewing but no such smells greeted his nose. Rolling out of his blankets Will carefully looked around and was flabbergasted by what he saw or more precisely by what he did not see. For there was no black horse, no mysterious rider, and no wagon. Will could not believe that Jack and Ellen could have harnessed the team and moved the wagon out while he slept. He began searching the area and was amazed to see that there were no tracks of any kind leaving the area. In fact, there were no tracks of any kind coming to the area except for one horse. He walked through the campsite looking for footprints and he found some but from all accounts, they belonged to him alone.

Will started to saddle Prince. He figured that there was no sense sitting here in the middle of nowhere waiting for Jack and Ellen to reappear out of nothing. He was just checking to make sure his cinch was tight when he heard what sounded like several horsemen riding hard in his direction. From his past experience, Will knew that it was prudent to be prepared so he stepped back away from his horse and loosened the hammer strap on his pistol.

Will relaxed slightly when he saw that the horsemen were led by none other than the large round man with a Sheriff's star on his chest. "Good morning Sheriff. I am surprised to see you here this morning. What can I do for you?"

"You can tell me where the woman and your friend with the black horse are."

"As you can see Sheriff they are not here unless perhaps you think I have them hidden in my saddlebags. You are welcome to take a look if you wish."

"Don't be smart with me boy. You left Whipple with them last night after it had gotten dark. This was about how far you could have made it before making camp. And yet when we mounted up and rode out this morning there was no sign of any tracks other than what I assume were made by your horse. I don't see how that wagon could have left town without making some pretty deep ruts. Now, where did they go?"

"Your guess is as good as mine. We made camp here last night and ate dinner together. I had a little philosophical talk with Jack and then turned in. When I woke up this morning the wagon, Ellen, Jack, and his horse were gone. I did not hear them leave in the night and I found no trace that they were ever here this morning. Now if you will excuse me I was about to hit the trail. I have been riding for a very long time and I would like to find a hospitable town where I can get a bath a shave and a decent meal. If you will remember you told me to leave your town before I could get any of those luxuries."

"Boy your tale sounds like something out of a storybook. Wagons and horses do not just disappear in the middle of nowhere without leaving tracks."

"And yet here you are, seeing the same things that I do. And what I am seeing is that it appears there never existed a wagon or a man on a black horse. It is as big a mystery to me as to you. Now as I have committed no crime, I would like to be on my way."

"Well, then since there appears that there never was a wagon, I guess you could not have dropped off four bodies of wanted men at our undertakers. And if that were the case then there would be no reward to forward to your location. You are free to go. Just keep riding away from Whipple."

"Would you mind telling me where the next town might be?"

"Just keep following this trail that doesn't exist. You will reach Salem by midday. I wouldn't mention anything about disappearing horses and wagons though. Those folks are a little touchy about the unknown."

The sun was high in the sky when Will rode into the little town. He quickly found the livery stable and with a gold coin secured lodging and feed for his horse. Then grabbing his saddlebags and the long gun he set off for the only hotel in Salem. With any luck, he would be able to get a shave a bath, and a room with a real bed. As he strode down the street he noticed that every hitching rail seemed to be filled with horses. He thought that was strange for such a small town and figured that something must be going on. Perhaps this was county fair time.

He finally reached the hotel and entered the lobby only to see that even here every seat was taken. Making his way to the front desk he inquired about the availability of a room and was told that he would not find a room anywhere in the entire town of Salem due to the execution that was due to take place later in the day. Everyone in the surrounding area had shown up to witness the burning of the witch.

Will could not believe his ears. "I guess I should have made the connection between the name Salem and witches but this is too surreal." He thought. He turned to the clerk behind the counter and asked him how often this type of thing happened in Salem.

"It has been quite a long time. Most of the witches were wiped out many years ago. If Cyrus had not come home and caught his wife casting spells with chicken innards she probably would have gotten away with it. Nobody is looking for witches anymore. In any event, you will not be able to find a room today and probably for tomorrow. This is a big event and everyone will want to hang around to talk about what they witnessed."

"So let me get this straight," Will replied. "A man accuses his wife of witchcraft and with no other evidence, she is found guilty and sentenced to death. Sounds kind of convenient if a man wanted to get rid of a cantankerous wife."

"Most women know better than to be cantankerous as you put it. They are taught to obey their men folks from the time they are little girls. By the time they are to be married off they are pretty obedient."

"So if they are trained that well, how does one of them become a witch? It seems highly unlikely to me that they would be allowed contact with someone of the dark arts."

"You are talking to the wrong person. I am just a simple hotel clerk. In any event, it is too late for argument. She is set to be burned in the lot behind the Sheriff's office in about an hour. I will be closing up here shortly so that I can go and see the fun."

Will could not believe what he had just heard. Watching a woman being burned while she is still alive was referred to as fun. He had to get out of this town immediately or he was afraid he might do something he would regret. All that lived in this world he had been sent to were barbarians.

He exited the hotel and headed back up the street that he had just come down. He needed to get Prince and ride out of this town. Hopefully, he would be able to find somewhere a little more civilized. This pattern of town jumping was becoming tiresome.

The liveryman was surprised to see Will again so soon. "I just got your horse fed and brushed down. I figured you would be staying at least until after the burning. It isn't every day you get to see a witch burned at the stake."

"I cannot believe you people. You act like murdering women is entertainment. What kind of barbarians are you? Get my horse I will be leaving as quickly as possible."

The liveryman led Prince out of the stall and then turned to Will. "Here he is but you will have to saddle him yourself. The festivities are going to start in a few minutes and I don't want to miss watching them light the pyre. It may be years before we catch another witch."

"Unbelievable," thought Will. He quickly saddled his horse, threw his saddlebags across the back of the saddle, and put his long gun into the scabbard. As a matter, of course, he checked his sidearm to make sure it was loaded and ready to go. Something told him that danger might be lurking and so he did not put the hammer strap on. And then he turned to head out of town in the opposite direction he had entered.

The street was empty but he could hear shouting coming from somewhere to his left. He assumed that was where the "festivities" were taking place. He had no desire to witness what these people seemed to think was entertainment and so he urged his horse to a higher pace. But Prince would not respond. Instead, he kept trying to turn to the left towards the sounds. No matter how hard Will tried he could not keep his horse from heading in the one direction that Will definitely did not want to go in. And so despite his best intentions, Will found himself approaching a ring made up of almost all men. In the center lashed to a pole stood a lovely nude woman. And around her feet was a high pile of wood.

The crowd was cheering and urging someone to "Light the bitch". The woman was not saying a word but she was looking directly at Will and he could hear her thoughts in his head. She was telling him to save her. But how could he or any lone man save someone when so many wanted her dead?

And then without even thinking he was pulling his rifle from its scabbard. Someone on a tall platform was lighting a torch and was getting ready to toss it into the pile of wood at the feet of the woman. And then his rifle spoke. The torch was cut in half and the lit portion fell down the back of the man setting his shirt on fire. He began screaming and trying to get down from the tower. In desperation, he finally threw himself to the ground and began rolling in the dirt. The smell of burnt flesh was strong in the air and Will wondered why this crowd was so intent on smelling more of it.

Will forced his horse through the outer ring of revelers. He had slid his rifle back in its scabbard but his pistol was loose in his holster. "Go home all of you. There will be no burning at the stake today." Will demanded.

"Stranger, you just bit off more than you can chew." This was spoken by a man with a star pinned to his shirt. "This witch was tried and convicted and I am here to carry out her sentence. Unless you want to join her you will ride on."

"I can't seem to do that," Bill stated. "By the way how old are you Sheriff?"

"What difference does that make? But for your information, I am 42. Why do you ask?"

"I just think you might be a little old to be believing in witches. Now untie the woman and let her go before someone else gets hurt."

Out of the corner of his eye, Will saw someone starting to reach for his gun. Like a flash, Will's hand swept downward, and before anyone even knew he was drawing his pistol spit lead. The gun flew from the man's hand as Will's bullet hit the cylinder. Will quickly turned back to the Sheriff before he could draw his weapon. "Now I do not like to repeat myself. Release the woman."

"She was tried and convicted. And she is going to burn this very day."

"Perhaps you are right. I cannot kill you all. But one thing is certain, Sheriff. You will not live to see her burn."

The Sheriff slowly raised his hands and started backing towards the pyre. He could see the truth in Will's eyes and he was not going to die just so a man could get rid of his wife. Carefully he drew a long knife and cut the ropes from the woman's feet and hands. She quickly made her way to the edge of the crowd and grabbed her dress that was lying on the ground. No one made any move to stop her, each one figuring that Will was looking directly at them and the bore of that pistol was pointing directly between their eyes.

The woman approached Will's horse and he reached down with his left hand and pulled her up behind him. Only then did Prince whirl and stretch out to his full running speed headed out of town.

As soon as he could Will cut off the regular road and made his way up into some big rocks. He figured that the Sheriff would be putting together a posse and would be coming after them. He hoped that he could find a way to hide their tracks from their pursuers. He kept a close watch on their back trail but did not see anyone coming after them. And when it began getting dark enough so that it was not safe to travel, he pulled his horse behind a huge boulder and made camp for the night. They did not start a fire for fear of discovery.

Not a word had been spoken between Will and the woman but now that they were dismounted she finally spoke. "I appreciate what you did for me back there. Now, what can I do to repay you?"

"I am not looking for payment of any kind. In fact, if I have to tell the truth, I have no idea what I was thinking at the time. If you are going to thank someone, thank my horse. It was his fault that I did not leave."

The woman looked at Will and started unfastening her dress. She had undone most of the buttons before Will finally was able to speak. "Please stop with the buttons. I did not help you for your body. Don't get me wrong you are a very beautiful woman and any man would be lucky to have you but not because you are indebted to him."

She walked over to his horse and removed his riding crop from his saddle. She returned and handed it to him. "If you don't want sex, then perhaps you would like to whip me. I bruise easily and you would not even have to exert yourself to mark me. Men seem to get great enjoyment from causing pain."

Will dropped the crop by his feet. "Look, I know that you have a reason for thinking the worst of men, but I do not want anything other than to see you safely away from Salem. Do you have any relatives that you could go to?"

"I don't want to argue with the man that saved me from burning to death. However, it has been my experience that men do not help women unless there is something in it for them. I do not have any money so the only things I have to offer are sex or allowing abuse. And I always pay my debts."

"So why don't you just tell me about how you got into the mess you were in? Why in the world would any intelligent people take you for a witch?"

"Are you so sure that I am not a witch?" she said with a smile.

"Reasonably," Will replied. "For one thing I don't believe there are such things as witches. And secondly, if you were what they said you were, why did you not just turn them all into croaking frogs or toads?"

"Maybe it was just easier for me to talk to your horse and convince him not to allow you to leave town."

"Why don't you try to get some sleep? I will stand watch for a while although I doubt they will try catching us in the dark."

Will found a notch between two boulders and settled his back into it. He turned his ears to the night sounds listening for anything that might be out of the ordinary. But all he heard was the sounds of crickets and somewhere far away an owl hooted. Despite his best efforts he was soon sound asleep.

Chapter Ten - The Second Trial

Will opened his eyes and knew that something was terribly wrong. He felt hard cold steel pressed to the side of his head and he knew that his falling asleep might well be the precursor of his permanent sleep. He turned his head as much as possible and saw that a man was holding Will's revolver to his head. Four other men were surrounding him while one man was holding a struggling convicted witch.

"Well, not so big now that we have pulled your teeth are you?" None other than the Sheriff he had buffaloed back in Salem spoke this.

"And you Mandy, did you really think I was going to let you just ride off into the sunset with another man?" The question was asked by the man that had tried to light the pyre only to have his own back burned when Will had shot the torch out of his hand.

"Why not Cyrus? Don't you have another woman now? Isn't that why you trumped up these phony charges?"

"You had your trial witch. Now it is time for you to burn. We have already prepared two pyres, one for you and one for your knight in shining armor. We are going to force him to watch you burn so he will see what it is like and then we will light him on fire. Tie him up boys and make sure he has a good point of view downwind. I am sure he will enjoy the smell."

Will's hands were quickly bound behind his back and Mandy was taken kicking and screaming to a tree that stood by itself in the clearing. She was stripped of her dress and her hands were tied behind her and around the trunk of the tree. A good supply of wood was already arranged around her. Will tried to struggle against his bonds but he was not able to free his hands. Then the Sheriff spoke. "Mandy you have been found guilty of the crime of witchcraft. You have been sentenced to burn at the stake. Do you have any last words?"

"You all know that the only reason I am here is that I caught Cyrus in bed with the town whore. Rather than allow me to just leave he trumped up this charge. I hope he catches a disease and his cock falls off."

The Sheriff then handed the torch to Cyrus. If you still want to do the honors go ahead and finish this.

As the torch was being lit, Will felt the ropes around his wrists starting to move. And then he heard a voice in his head. "Throw the ropes at them, Will." It said.

Just then the ropes came all the way undone and dropped into his open palms. But for some reason, they no longer felt like ropes. They were wriggling and moving about and Will had a tremendous urge to get rid of them. Following the voice in his head, Will launched the ropes toward the Sheriff and the man called Cyrus. In mid-flight, he saw that they were indeed not ropes but rather deadly serpents. They struck the two men just above the shoulders and coiled themselves around their necks sinking their fangs into their faces. With a cry of desperation, the two men fell to the ground.

In the ensuing panic caused by the strange sight, Will grabbed his pistol from the man next to him. He used it to strike the man behind his ear and as he fell to the ground unconscious Will retrieved his gun belt. The other members of the posse were all running for cover. The sport of witch-burning was now becoming far too dangerous for them.

Will was completely shocked by what had taken place. He walked over to the Sheriff and Cyrus and inspected them. Neither man showed any signs of being bitten by a snake. And the only thing lying on the ground near them was the ropes that had bound Will's hands. But the two men were indeed dead. Their faces were white as ghosts and if Will was a betting man he would wager they had died of fright. Now if he could only rectify what he had seen. Were the serpents merely illusions or had they been changed back after they had done their work?

Mandy walked over to him. "We should probably be going. I doubt that there will be any more coming after us, but I would feel better if we put some distance between Salem and us. I will take Cyrus' horse so we will not have to ride double. If the ones that ran come back they can put both bodies across one horse and take them back to town."

"I agree but where will we go? Unless there is a town where the people are not barbarians we are destined to ride forever on the range."

"Well, a man and his wife can travel anywhere they want without trouble," Mandy said with a smile.

"Whoa, woman, I don't know if I am ready to marry a witch even one as beautiful as you."

"How old are you Will Anderson?"

"I don't rightly know in this life," Will replied. "Why?"

"I was just thinking that you might be a little too old to be believing in witches." And Mandy broke out laughing as she mounted her horse.

Part Two
The Cowboy Takes A Lady
Chapter Eleven - Getting Acquainted

Will Anderson looked over at the beautiful raven-haired woman riding next to him and marveled at how they had met. He had saved her, or more accurately perhaps, his horse, Prince, had saved her from being roasted at a local witch-burning regalia. He had ridden into the small town of Salem simply looking for a good meal and a bed for the night only to find the town brimming with excitement and flooded with people. Once he had found that there were no rooms available to be had and the reason for the overflow of people he mounted his horse and tried to ride out of that town. He had no desire to become involved in yet another mess that was clearly none of his business. But for some reason, his horse would not allow him to leave until he was in up to his hat in a hornet's nest. A few non-lethal shots were fired and the lady had been freed and had swung up behind his saddle and Prince was galloping out of town leaving stunned, disappointed residents and a cloud of dust.

That should have been the end of it. Will planned to make sure the woman was safely out of harm's way and then proceed to parts unknown. But a bitter husband and a red-faced Sheriff had other ideas. They had chased them down and again the woman was tied to a tree with a pile of wood at her feet. And this time Will was tied to another tree with his own pile of wood ready to be lit. What had happened next, Will was still trying to figure out. Ropes that bound him had miraculously turned into serpents and one vindictive Sheriff and one evil husband lay dead. Their cause of death was still speculation. They might have died from snakebite or more likely had been scared to death. In either case, the rest of the crowd had developed a healthy respect for their intended victims and had withdrawn post-haste leaving Will and Mandy free to ride again unmolested.

The sun was rapidly descending and Will looked for a good spot to make camp for the night. He reined his horse to a stop under two large oak trees and looked in all directions. And then for the first time since she had vaulted into her saddle, the woman spoke.

"It looks like there is a small cave on the side of the next hill. That might provide us with some shelter from the cold tonight. Will raised his arm to shield his eyes from the setting sun and peered into the distance but for the life of him, he was unable to see the cave, which she spoke of.

Mandy did not wait for him, she simply set off at a lope toward the hill she had mentioned. Having no better idea in mind, Will followed but kept his eyes open for any sign of trouble. He had realized that little else existed in this brutal land.

By the time Will caught up to her Mandy was already off of her horse and heading for the mouth of the cave. "Hey, wait for me," He hollered after her. "Hadn't this woman learned anything from almost being burned at the stake twice in the last 24 hours?" He thought to himself.

She stopped and looked back at him with a big smile on her face. She watched as he dismounted and then grinned a little more as he undid the safety strap from the hammer of his pistol.

"Don't worry." She announced. "There is no danger here. I would sense it if there were."

"You didn't sense that posse catching me sleeping back there. That little lapse almost got us both roasted if you remember."

Again Mandy smiled at him. You only assume that I did not sense them. Perhaps I just did not want to have to look over my shoulder at that evil man for the rest of my life and I wanted to end his hatefulness.

Will had not even considered that possibility and once again he had to reevaluate everything that had happened since he had met her. He was still standing with his mouth half-open when she turned and headed into the cave. "See if you can find us some firewood. There is a good place to make a fire for cooking and warmth in here."

Shaking his head in wonder, Will checked his surroundings. He was not surprised in the least that there was a plentitude of downed trees, apparently from some large storm that had passed through some time ago. Will was cautious as he moved the dead limbs, making sure that no serpents were lurking underneath. He did not have any tools for cutting the wood so he only took what looked small and brittle enough that he could break. He dragged a couple of long limbs to the cave entrance and then returned for more.

Will was surprised that by the time he had returned Mandy had already started the fire and had begun preparing an evening meal. He had no idea where the food had come from and he was curious but the subject could wait until later.

After they had finished eating, Will got his bedroll and spread it out a little ways from the fire. "You can sleep there for the night."

"And where will you sleep, dear Knight?"

"I need to stand guard anyway. I would rather not wake up with a gun to my head, in the morning."

"Trust me we will be safe tonight. Nobody is following us anymore and besides the horses will alert us should anyone stumble across this cave. Crawl under the blankets with me and let's share our body heat. I promise you that I will not bite."

As tired as Will was, the offer was tempting, but something in the back of his mind would not let him accept. He dragged both of the saddles inside the cave; set hers on the ground at the head of the bedroll and his against the wall closest to the fire. He watched her as she slid under the blankets, still fully clothed. Then he lay down with his head on his saddle and pulled his saddle blanket over him for warmth.

Although he planned on being watchful his eyes were soon closed and a soft snoring sound emanated from his lips. The night passed quickly and soon he awoke to the smell of coffee brewing and something delicious cooking in the frying pan.

Chapter Twelve - Morning Visitors

"It is about time you rolled out of your bed." The woman said with a smile. "You just have enough time to eat and have a cup of coffee before our guests arrive."

With a feeling of trepidation, Will asked Mandy what guests those might be and if there was cause for concern.

"They have come for me, I imagine. So, if you are worried about your safety perhaps you should just turn me over to them and your worries will be over."

"Is your opinion of me so low as to think that I would simply hand you over to face God only knows what kind of horrors? Haven't I proved anything to you yet?"

"Frankly I have not figured out exactly what you want out of this arraignment. I offered you the only two things I have as repayment for your services and you have turned both down. Even my offer to share body heat with you was rejected. But, let's talk later. Now eat and drink and we will see what these men want that are coming up the crease."

Will had just finished eating a plate of eggs and drinking a cup of coffee when he heard someone yell, "Hello, the camp. We are coming in."

Will has already removed the hammer strap from his sidearm and had checked to make sure that all six cylinders had fresh loads in them. He moved slightly to his left making sure that a large boulder was at his back before answering. "Come on in but keep your hands out in the open where I can see them. And I am the nervous sort so don't make any quick movements that I might mistake for hostility."

In a single file, three men stepped into the clearing. They slowly fanned out making themselves more difficult targets for a lone gunman. The one in the center was a large man. The huge mustache he wore made him look like an old-time gunfighter Will had seen in some of the movies he had enjoyed when he was young. A shiny star was pinned on the left side of his shirt and Will wondered exactly how many Sheriffs there might be in this land.

"What do I owe this visit too?" Will asked no one in particular although he was sure the Sheriff would be the one to answer.

"We have come for the woman." The Sheriff declared.

"Women must be mighty scarce in this part of the country," Will replied. "Why almost everywhere I go someone is wanting my woman."

"Perhaps that is the problem. There is some question about her ownership. And looking at her I don't see a collar around her neck, nor are there hobbles on her feet."

Will expected Mandy to chime in with a sharp retort at any moment but the woman remained quiet. So Will shot back his reply.

"Does she look like a dog to you Sheriff? Or perhaps you think she might be a horse. Where I come from men do not treat their women as animals."

"What she looks like is a dangerous female." The Sheriff spat back. "And I will feel a whole lot safer once I have her in chains."

"I am afraid that will not happen as long as I stand between her and you. The woman belongs to me and my guns are primed and ready to protect her."

"Stranger I have heard about a man matching your description. Some say you are faster than greased lightning with that sidearm of yours. But as you can see there are three of us. Even for a man of your reputation that might be long odds. Either produce the proper papers showing us that the woman is rightfully yours or step aside and allow me to do my job."

For the first time, Will was stumped. He did not know any papers that would be necessary to prove his claim. Perhaps they were asking for a wedding certificate but if so Will did not have one. Will wanted to divert his eyes to look at Mandy but he knew that would be all the opening the big man and his deputies would need to draw their weapons and begin shooting.

"Will, I have the papers he requires. Should I give them to him?" Mandy asked.

Now, Will was totally confused. He knew of no such papers so how could Mandy have them? But he decided to play along to see where this was going. "Mandy there is a big rock in the right of center in the clearing. Put the papers on that but make sure you do not come between the Sheriff and me. And Sheriff make sure your men understand that if there is any gunplay you will be the first one to swallow a piece of lead."

Will watched cautiously as Mandy made her way into the clearing carrying a sheaf of papers. She set them down on the rock and then quickly backed out of the line of fire.

The Sheriff eased over to the rock, picked up the documents, and began reading them silently. His expression went from one of disbelief to one of great anger. His face became so red that his mustache seemed to be giving off a little smoke. By this time Will was really curious. "Would you mind reading aloud Sheriff? You seem to be having a little trouble understanding the wording. Perhaps reading out loud will clarify the meaning."

The Sheriff cleared his throat and then began reading. "This is to certify that Will Anderson, being of sound mind and body has agreed to take possession of one Amanda Wilkes. He agrees to provide such a person with protection until either his death, infirmity, or until he grows tired of her. If the later occurs he will be responsible for transferring ownership to another adult male."

"So what seems to be the trouble Sheriff?" Will asked. "It sounds like everything is in order."

"Yes, right down to the proper seals. But I had it on good authority that this woman was not under the proper ownership of a male. And further that she might be wanted for crimes against humanity. Perhaps the two of you should come with me until we get this straightened out. If you would kindly lay down your weapons and lead the way to your horses."

"Sheriff, I have had quite enough of this persecution. You asked for documentation, which has been provided. Clearly, your information was inaccurate. And I have no intention of giving up my guns. My temper is running short so either back on out of here the way you came or reach for the gun you wear."

The Sheriff started to speak but Will was finished with the conversation. In a blur his hand went to his side and before the Sheriff even realized he had started to draw he was staring down the muzzle of a .375 magnum. The Sheriff knew this was not the time to make a point and he started backing slowly out of the clearing. His three deputies followed. When he was out of sight he called back. "This is not over. We will be waiting for you."

"You better make sure of your aim if you plan to back shoot me. I will not be giving any more warnings. The next time I draw I will shoot to kill."

Will followed them to make sure that they moved out of gun range. Then he returned to the clearing to find that Amanda had already packed their belongings and was in the process of saddling their horses.

"There are some things to talk about," Will announced, "but I guess they will have to wait until we find a way out of this mess. I am positive that sheriff is setting up an ambush for us when we go back out toward the main trail."

"Then I guess we should not go back the way we came."

"Do you know of another way?" Will asked as he looked around him not seeing another trail.

"Yes, there is an old game trail that leads up and around the top of this hill. It is hard to see because it has grown over with brush but we should be able to follow it with a little help from some friends up above."

Will looked up to the sky and could see what appeared to be a Red-Tailed Hawk gliding above them. The bird's screech seemed to have meaning for his female companion and Will shook his head in wonder. Could this remarkable woman communicate with the bird above?

Chapter Thirteen - The Escape

The trail was indeed narrow and grown over and they had to lead the horses to stay on it. It took a winding route around the hill constantly working itself toward the top. Will had no idea exactly where it lead but he could see Amanda checking the bird above them from time to time and she seemed confident that she was being pulled in the right direction.

Several times they stopped to rest themselves and the horses before again starting up the steep incline. The higher they climbed the more the trail widened as less and less brush could grow on the thinner soil. Soon the trail had turned to shale and they had to be careful that their horses did not slip on it.

And then they reached the top where the ground was almost all hard rock. The view was an absolute panorama of beauty in all directions. Will checked down their back-trail to see if he could detect anyone that might be following them but he saw nothing that made him suspicious. He could see far back in the distance a waft of smoke rising from where he figured they had started and discerned that the sheriff and his posse had probably made camp for the night.

"We are going to need a place with some water and I doubt we will find it at this elevation. We only have a couple of hours before sunset so we better push on down the hill a way and hoped to find water."

"Not to worry. Our feathered friend will lead us to water." And with that Amanda led the way off of the mountaintop.

It was not long before they were again entering a wooded area. Here they found more adult trees and less brush and only occasionally did they catch a glimpse of the hawk floating on the air stream above them. Several times Will caught sight of game slipping away out in front of him and he was sure that there would be water somewhere close by. The screeching of the bird above interrupted his thoughts, and Amanda reined her horse sharply to the right and towards a thick clump of bushes that seemed to grow almost out of the side of the hill.

It was almost dark but from the way, his horse nickered Will was sure that water was close at hand. Amanda dismounted and led her horse to the thick growth. As Will followed suit Prince immediately started forward and it was all Will could do to maintain control of the animal.

"There is a small pool of water here but there is only enough room for one horse at a time. When Nell finishes drinking I will back out and allow you and Prince to come forward."

With some effort, Will was able to restrain his thirsty horse. As Amanda and her mount backed out Will led Prince into the narrow opening and to the small pool of water. It appeared to originate from a rock wall and the overflow formed a small creek cascading down the side of the mountain. Will observed copious amounts of animal tracks and he figured that this pool was the central watering hole for most of the animals that lived in the area. When his horse had drunk his fill Will led him back out into the forested area and removed his saddle. Using his saddle blanket Will wiped the horse down and then picketed him where there was plenty of tender green grass for him to crop.

By the time Will returned to the campsite a meal of bacon, beans, and coffee awaited him. "I think it is time we had a little talk about the strange things that are happening around here," Will announced.

"Specifically what strange things are you referring to?" Amanda shot back.

"Well, for starters how did you know that the sheriff and his posse would be coming at the exact time they arrived?"

"That was easy. I heard the excitement and fear of the animals and the birds as those men made their way toward our camp. And I suppose you were wondering about the hawk leading us to the trail up the mountain?"

"I did find that a might strange but I suppose you have some logical explanation for it?"

"In fact I do. I figured that hawk would be keeping an eye on the game trails and if I watched closely enough he would lead me to one that was well-used. So I just watched closely to see what he was looking at."

"I am not sure that I buy that one."

"Then perhaps you would like to come up with a better explanation. Maybe you think that I can converse with the birds of prey?"

"No more than I believe that you had a conversation with my horse back in Salem," Will said tongue in cheek. "Now maybe you can explain where the bacon came from that you are cooking up in that pan?"

"Why, I do believe that it came from the same place that all bacon comes from, a pig." And Amanda could not help but allow a small laugh to escape her lips even though she tried hard not to.

"You know what I am asking. I don't recall seeing a pig hung over your saddle."

"No, but perhaps there might have been part of a pig in my saddlebags. Did you ever think of that?"

"Yes, I have been thinking about a lot of things. For instance, where did you get those papers that you gave the sheriff this morning? I don't remember attending any ceremony where I agree to become your protector."

"People often see what they are expecting to see. The sheriff asked for our wedding papers and when I gave them to him he expected that they would be what he asked for."

"I am not buying that one. For one thing, he read my name out loud. If it had not been there how would he have known what it was? Or your name for that matter?"

"News travels fast in this part of the world. I am sure that where ever we go people will have heard of us."

"So we are destined to have to run from the law everywhere we go? Is that what you are saying?"

"Well, you could always go through with the ceremony and take me for your own. Then you would have the correct papers to present to any law enforcement personnel that might ask for them. Or you could just turn me over to the next sheriff we meet and be done with me. But while you are mulling over your decision I suggest we have something to eat and then turn in for the night. And we will not have a cave to keep the wind out tonight so you might want to decide if you have enough courage to share the blankets with a witch tonight."

Will did not have to think about whether or not he wanted to turn Mandy over to the local sheriff or anyone else for that matter. He had not gone through all that he had just to put her back into a situation that might be worse than the one he had extricated her from. And besides, he had come to enjoy her company. He doubted that in two lifetimes he had ever met a woman that had so much life and intrigue. And at that moment Will discovered something that he had been trying to avoid. It was a definite possibility that he was falling in love with this strange and beautiful woman.

As night approached Mandy again urged Will to share her blankets. We do not have a cave tonight to shelter us from the wind. I imagine that we will need all the warmth we can get. It only makes sense that we share each others.

Will reluctantly agreed and still wearing his clothing he slipped in beside her. As he put his arm around her to draw her close to him he was shocked to discover that unlike him Mandy was stark naked. He pulled his arm back so fast that he threw the blankets off of both of them.

"Oh dear lord in heaven. Why in the world did you do that? The air is freezing. Give me back my blankets."

"Look, Mandy, I am sorry."

"Don't you say another word, Will Anderson. We are not having this conversation tonight. Perhaps tomorrow you can explain to me why you find me so unattractive that just touching me causes you to recoil, but not tonight."

That was the first time that Will had ever seen Mandy that angry. Even when she had been faced with death at the hands of her evil husband her voice had not carried that amount of bitterness. He knew better than to try and explain himself to her when she was that upset and so he grabbed his saddle blanket, moved over as close to the dying fire as he could, and tried to go to sleep. It was one of the longest nights of his life.

Chapter Fourteen - Making a New Friend

Sometime in the middle of the night some of the chill left Will's body and he fell into a deep and dreamless sleep. The sun was high in the sky before he awoke to someone wiping his face with a warm, wet, and coarse cloth. He put up his hand to ward them off only to have it come in contact with something wet attached to something very furry.

Something was not right but Will's mind was still foggy from sleep. But when that rag again started washing his face his eyes came completely open. What he saw made him jump up and back away from the biggest white wolf he had ever seen. The creature seemed to be smiling at him but the huge fangs dripping saliva did not look friendly in the least. From instinct, he reached for his revolver and had it half drawn when he heard Mandy's voice.

"Don't you dare hurt that poor animal. He is just trying to wake you up. The morning is half gone and we should be moving down the trail to someplace a little warmer. It looks like there might be some snow moving into this high country.

Will was still unsure of the wolf but he trusted Mandy's instincts about animals. He slowly backed away from the wolf and made his way to where Prince was busily cropping the tender grass. He slipped the bridle over the horse's ears and then began leading him to the spring for a drink of water while Will washed the wolf's saliva from his face. With some trepidation, Will noticed that the huge canine was following them and he made sure that the hammer strap was loosened from his side-arm.

Reaching the spring, Will allowed his horse to drink his fill before approaching the water himself. He looked back to where the wolf sat on his haunches but the big dog-like creature did not seem to be posing any threat. Will moved to the far side of the pool where he could keep an eye on the wolf and then watchfully bent down and scooped up a handful of water. He splashed it on his face and then got another and repeated the action.

Finally satisfied that his face was as clean as it was going to get, he allowed himself to drink deeply from the cold sweet water. He then moved down the trail away from the spring to do his morning ablutions. Only when Will had vacated his spot by the stream did the wolf move in to slake his own thirst.

When the trio returned to the campsite Will was not in the least surprised to smell fresh coffee and hear the sizzling sounds of bacon in a pan. Will had come to accept the marvelous talents that the beautiful dark-haired beauty possessed. And one of those talents was making coffee and food appear.

Will poured himself a cup and took a small sip relishing the rich flavor and aroma of the brew. Never in his life had he tasted a better cup of coffee and he remarked that thought to Mandy. She did not reply but her smile was enough for Will to understand that she deeply appreciated his compliment.

As Will filled his plate with eggs and bacon from the pan the wolf again appeared and sat on his haunches looking at Will and his plate of food longingly. The coal-black eyes seemed to be staring deep into Will's soul and his lips dripped with saliva as if he was either dreaming of taking Will's food or taking Will for food. A small shine emanated from behind those large sharp teeth and Will began to feel guilty for not sharing his breakfast with his uninvited guest.

Will looked at Mandy and saw that she had a large grin on her face.

"Don't let Caesar push a guilt trip onto you." She remarked. "He is perfectly capable of catching his breakfast. But of course, if you are foolish enough to fall for his begging, he will take any charity offered.

"Caesar huh?"

Mandy looked at him curiously. "Yes, Caesar. That is his name. Why don't you think he looks like royalty?"

I am not sure what a royal wolf looks like. But just how did you know his name or did you just decide to give him one?"

Maybe he told me. You do believe that I can talk with animals don't you?"

Will thought back to his horse refusing to leave town until they had rescued Mandy and then to the hawk flying up above them and apparently showing them the way up the mountainside. But he wasn't willing to absolutely accept that Mandy had caused those things. "Why don't you tell me where Caesar came from?"

"Oh, he just showed up sometime during the night and snuggled up next to you as if he had been doing it his entire life. And it is probably a good thing he did as your stupid pride might have caused you to freeze to death. I suppose this is as good a time as any to get this conversation over with. Just what is it about me that repulses you so much that you cannot stand to touch me?"

"Of for heaven's sakes, Mandy. You know that you do not repulse me in any way. It is just that you seem duty-bound to offer me your body out of some debt you believe you owe me. I told you that first night we were together that I did not expect any form of payment for what I did to help you out of that fix you were in."

"And just what made you think that I was offering my body to you last night? Isn't it possible that I just wanted to share a little body heat so that we could both stay warm?"

"We could have shared our body heat just as well if you had kept your clothes on under those blankets."

"I see this conversation is going nowhere, so we might as well head down the trail.

Will waited until Mandy was in her saddle before putting his foot into the stirrup and swinging up onto Prince's back. He admired how her small bottom fit into her saddle as he watched her horse make his way down the mountainside. For a small woman, she sure had a big impact on him and he wondered if he might be falling for her.

Chapter Fifteen - Is it Love or is it Lust

As they descended further down the mountain, Will noticed that the temperature began to warm. Occasionally he would see the flash of a deer's tail or a rabbit scurrying through the brush and he wondered if Caesar had indeed decided to hunt for his breakfast. The wolf had disappeared as quietly as he had appeared in camp.

They had been riding for perhaps three hours when they came out of the heavy woods. Will could hear the sound of rapidly moving water and he realized that they were close to a large stream or river. Before them lay a huge grassy plain with scattered fruit trees. It seemed to Will that they had suddenly come upon the Garden of Eden and he wondered if there was a tree with forbidden fruit somewhere within his view.

Mandy stopped her horse and dismounted just on the edge of the meadow. "This looks like a great spot to rest the horses and my bottom." She announced. "I believe there is a river just a little way off to our left. Why don't you take the horses over for a drink while I gather some of the fruit available and start a fire for coffee?"

Will led the horses in the direction of the sound of running water. It was more a small river than a stream and Will was taken with its' beauty. Large pools gathered where rocks had been placed randomly in the river bed and Will could see the flashing bodies of fish as they came to the surface for the insects that came for a drink. Wishing he had a fishing pole Will Led the horses to a quiet spot at the edge of the river and allowed them to drink their fill.

As Will waited for the horses to finish he looked across the river and there sitting on his haunches was Caesar. His white coat had splotches of red, especially around his muzzle and Will knew that Mandy had been right. Caesar certainly could find his own breakfast. The big wolf dipped his nose into the water, took a drink, and then plunged into the current. He was a powerful swimmer and in a matter of seconds, he had traversed the water and came out on Will's side a little upstream.

Will wondered why the wolf insisted on staying close. He certainly did not look like a domesticated animal. But just the same Will was no longer fearful of the big carnivore. In fact, his presence brought some degree of comfort to him.

Realizing that he had not eaten in quite a few hours, Will led the horses away from the river and headed back to where he had left Mandy. She was never one to disappoint and she had an entire meal prepared including fresh fruit that she had gathered from the variety of trees in the meadow.

She beckoned to a fallen log and Will knew that she was indicating his seat at the dinner table. Will marveled at the fact that he had not gone without food since he had met this amazing woman. It was certainly an upgrade in lifestyle from the days just after awakening from that cave somewhere many miles ago.

Mandy smiled as she watched him eat the meal she had prepared. She thought how pleasant it was to be in the company of a man that appreciated her culinary talents even if he did not seem to appreciate her sexual charms. Well, she guessed she would take whatever small favors she could get.

"Do you think we should stay here for a day or two and give the horses some rest?" Mandy brought Will back to the present.

"That might be a good idea. I don't think there is any place we need to be in a hurry. In fact, I have no idea where we are headed. Has your hawk given you any indication about that?"

"I don't have a hawk. No one owns the wild creatures of this world." Her voice seemed to carry some annoyance and Will was not sure why.

"Since you have no objection to hanging around here for a day or so, I think I will find a place to wash the trail dust from my hair and body. I am sure you can find something to do around here while I am gone."

"Do you think it a good idea for you to go off by yourself? I have no idea what or who might happen by."

"I am sure I will be fine but if you think I need protection, I will invite Caesar to go with me."

Will looked in her direction and he noticed that the big wolf was already by her side. "He looks like he is willing to be your knight in shining armor."

Will watched Mandy walking away and again appreciated the view of her small bottom as it swayed back and forth tantalizingly. He felt his body responding to the view and he felt a little guilty since he had repeatedly rejected her advances. If only those advances were not because of some mistaken feeling of gratitude.

Will shook his head to get the carnal thoughts out of his mind. Then he busied himself with finding firewood to last them through the night. He checked the sky and could find no sign of rain on the horizon so he did not figure he needed to erect some type of crude shelter. If the wind stayed calm they would be comfortable enough right here under what promised to be a clear and starlit night.

Mandy had been gone for what Will thought was an inordinate amount of time and so he started toward where he had last seen her. He again arrived at the bank of the river but Mandy was nowhere to be found. He checked the stream bank and found some tracks where she had walked along the riverbank upstream. Her footprints were not hard to follow nor did there seem to be any other prints other than those left by the wolf so Will had little trepidation as he followed them.

He had gone a little more than perhaps a quarter of a mile when he saw what looked like steam coming up from the ground a short way from the far bank of the river. Will also noticed that Mandy's tracks entered the river at this point. Not wanting to ruin his boots, Will removed them, lashed them together with the bootstrings, and slung them over his shoulder before stepping into the current.

The steam seemed to become thicker, the closer he got to it. There was some thick brush surrounding the area where Will believed the steam emanated from. Not knowing what he might find he quietly moved through the brush. He was still inside the edge of the brush when he got a glimpse of what was on the inside of it.

Will's mouth dropped open as he watched Mandy step out of what appeared to be a hot spring. Her long black hair cascaded down past her shoulders and obscured the view of what he was sure would be perfectly shaped breasts. But that hair did nothing to obscure the magnificent body below those breasts. And Will was not the only being that was enjoying the view. From every branch of the surrounding trees, wild birds gathered and warbled their appreciation for the beauty before them.

Caesar too sat on his haunches with his large mouth hanging open. Then for a reason that Will could not understand the wolf rose and walked away into the forest beyond the rising steam. Mandy had now picked up her shirt and had begun toweling the water droplets that still clung to her naked body.

Will was totally immersed in watching the beautiful woman and his manhood would have stood straight up and at attention if it had not been constrained by the denim of his jeans.

"Are you enjoying the view?" Mandy's voice brought him back to reality.

"I don't know about him but we certainly are." A strange voice replied.

Will had been so engrossed in the scene before him that he had not noticed the three men that had apparently followed his and Mandy's tracks. He could not believe that he had not heard them approach or that Mandy had not sensed their presence.

Will started to reach for the gun at his hip but that voice stopped him. "I would not do that if I was you. You have three rifles pointed at your stomach. I wouldn't want you dying of lead poisoning before you have the chance to watch what we are going to do to your woman."

Will thought he might have a chance to draw and fire before one of them got a shot off but probably not all three. And besides Mandy might be hit by a stray bullet and that thought slowed him down considerably.

"Now missy, drop the shirt and move that hair back behind your shoulders and give us a look at those tits of yours."

Will felt his ire rising and it was all he could do to stop himself from what might be a fatal mistake. He knew that he needed some type of distraction if he was going to have any possibility of getting out of this fix.

"Why don't you come over here and move the hair yourself? Or aren't you man enough to take control of a real woman?"

Will did not know why Mandy was goading the man. He obviously did not need any encouragement in what he was planning.

"Well, well, well. I think we have a live one boys. Keep her man covered while I go sample the merchandise."

"Just as long as you leave some for us when you are finished." Another voice remarked.

Will had managed to turn slowly enough so that he had not drawn attention to himself. He now had a clear view of all three men. They looked like old-time mountain men with their hair unkempt and their beards untrimmed. Their deerskin clothing did not look like it had been washed in years and Will could almost smell their body odor from 15 feet away. The one that had spoken first took a couple of quick steps toward Mandy. He reached out with his right hand when the distraction that Will needed took place.

The man's hand had just made contact with Mandy's hair when a white blur hit him from the side and drove him to the ground. He lost his rifle when he fell and all he could do was move his arm between the wolf's teeth and his throat.

His companions switched their attention from Will desperately trying to get a clean shot at Caesar. That proved to be a fatal mistake as Will's pistol jumped into his hand and two bullets left the barrel on a deadly flight toward two would-be rapists. Will's aim was deadly and both bullets found their mark in fatal organs.

Will walked over to where the two lay, making sure that they were dead. Just to be safe he picked up their rifles and tossed them into the brush as far as he could throw them. He then turned his attention to Mandy and was glad to see that she had managed to retrieve her shirt and put it on. Now he could see what he could do for the third outlaw.

It had only been moments since the wolf had taken the outlaw down but it was already too late to save the man. Caesar had already moved away from him but Will could see that he had not left until he had ripped the man's throat open. Great volumes of blood had spurted from the open wound and the man was already dead from loss of blood.

Will turned back to Mandy and saw that a tear was slowly making itself down from the corner of each eye. This was the first time that Will had seen the woman show this much emotion and he moved quickly to her and took her in his arms pulling her head against his chest.

"None of this is your fault," Will told her as he stroked her back.

"It is, though," Mandy replied. "If I had not been so engrossed in trying to arouse your passion I would have known those three were coming and we could have gotten the drop on them instead of having to kill them."

Will thought about that for a moment before replying. "And what would we have done with them if we had taken them alive? I don't know if there is a town with an honest sheriff close to here and even if there was what punishment would they have received if we stopped them before they tried to rape you. So we would just have had to release them so that they could try again with you or some other innocent woman. Make no mistake, the world is a better place without those three in it."

Even with his encouraging words, Mandy broke down and cried into his shirt. All he could do was slowly rub circles against her shoulder blades and kiss away the tears from her face. When she had finally composed herself Will allowed her to finish dressing while he moved the bodies well away from the water. He did not have a shovel, so trying to bury them was out of the question. All he could do is try to cover them with dead limbs and brush that could be found in abundance. He had no idea whether that would be enough to keep animals or birds away from the bodies and truthfully he did not care a lot. Those three did not deserve any compassion as far as he was concerned.

Mandy had still not composed herself by the time Will had helped her back to the campsite. He settled her on the ground with her back against a fruit tree and then he wrapped her in a blanket as he was afraid that she might go into shock.

He dragged firewood over close to where she sat and set about making a fire. He noticed that her sobs had stopped but she was still shaking under the blanket. His heart went out to her. He had never seen her so vulnerable and it broke his heart.

By the time the fire was going well and he had coffee started some of the color had returned to Mandy's face. Handing her a cup of coffee he kept his hand under the cup to make sure that she did not drop it. Finally, she managed to raise the cup by herself to her mouth and took a small sip. She offered him a small smile giving him hope that perhaps she would come back to her normal brave self.

"Why does God allow such evil to exist in this world?" She asked with a quaver in her voice."

"I wish I had a good answer to your question. I had this conversation with a man that was far more familiar with God's ways than I am. He said it was a matter of "free will"."

"What is that supposed to mean?" Amanda asked.

"I am not completely sure, but I guess it means that God allows each of us to make our own decisions. I wonder however if perhaps the evil ones have more free will than the righteous ones."

Mandy just shook her head and then took another sip of her coffee. It was obvious to Will that she did not completely grasp the concept of what he had told her, but he had no better answer than the one he had given.

The night was rapidly approaching and Will was setting up a spot for Mandy to sleep when she spoke to him. "Just for tonight would you please hold me as we sleep? I know you don't want to touch me but I really need to feel your arms around me."

"You have no idea how much I want to touch you." Will thought but did not say it out loud. He helped Mandy to lie down and then crawled under the blankets with her. He drew her back against him and felt her snuggle contentedly against his body. Her bottom was resting against him in just the wrong place and he felt his body responding he knew that it was going to be a long sleepless night for him. Mandy, on the other hand, had already lapsed into a peaceful sleep.

At some point during the night, Caesar returned and lay beside Will. Only when he realized the big wolf was there to offer comfort did Will drift off into a fitful sleep.

Chapter Sixteen - A Quest for a Safer Place

By the time that Will awoke Mandy was already up and had the coffee started. Will reluctantly rolled out from under the blankets and without a thought, to himself, he walked over to where the black-haired beauty was busy making breakfast. He cleared his throat to let her know of his presence before putting his arms around her and pulling her into a tight embrace. He gave her a light kiss on her cheek and was rewarded by feeling her body relax and settle back against him. He now knew that he had fallen in love with her but was unable to say those words to her out of fear that she might reject them thinking that they were not sincere but merely pity.

"This feels really good." She said to him. "However if you want to eat sometime this morning you might want to let me go. Take the horses for water and do what you need to. By the time you return we can eat and talk about where we will go from here."

He wanted to ask her how she was feeling, but he did not want to dredge up the terrible memories from yesterday until she was ready to talk about them on her own. So he gave her another light kiss on the cheek and set off to water the horses. He had no idea whether this was an area frequented by outlaws and so he removed the hammer strap from his pistol just in case.

Except for the birds chirping out their morning greeting everything was quiet as Will led the horses to the river. As he allowed them to drink their fill he looked around wondering if he would see the big wolf watching him, but there was not a hint of him.

As quickly as possible he finished his morning routine and headed back to camp. He noticed that their friendly hawk was soaring high in the sky as if he too was keeping a watch on Mandy. Every once in a while he would let out a loud screech and Will wished that he knew what that meant.

The sky was perfectly clear, not even a wisp of a cloud anywhere on the horizon. "This should be a good day for travel." He thought to himself.

Mandy handed Will a plate of food and then they both went to the downed log to sit and eat. She did not speak until Will had cleaned his plate of the last morsel and had finished his cup of coffee as well. Only then did she express the thoughts in her mind.

"It is a shame we have to leave this beautiful place." She began. "But I don't think that I can stand to be this close to the violence of yesterday."

"I agree, but unfortunately I do not know where we are or where we should go. You mentioned that you had a family somewhere. Could we go there?"

"My family is the last people that I want to see!" She exclaimed. "They are the ones that sold me to that monster that tried to burn me alive. And trust me, they would do it again if they thought they could get two gold coins for their trouble."

"Well, we need to find some type of civilization so that we can replenish our supplies. Maybe you could talk with your hawk friend and he could show us the way."

As Will said this he looked to see Mandy's reaction and was rewarded with a big smile. "You still think that I can converse with the animal kingdom, don't you?"

"I have come to realize that you can do almost anything you set your mind to." He replied. "But in any regard, I think that we can find some type of settlement if we just follow the river downstream. There is bound to be a town or village somewhere near the banks of that river."

Within a short period of time, the horses were saddled and Will and Mandy had mounted and headed towards the sound of the water. They swung their horses in the direction the water was flowing, keeping their eyes peeled for any sign of a trail or road that might lead them toward civilization.

They stayed close to the river to make sure that they were always headed downstream. If they were going to find a settlement of some kind it would be in that direction. The disadvantage of staying close to the river was that it did not travel in a straight line. It meandered all over the place turning to the right and then back to the left. This added a good many miles to their travels.

The sun was high in the sky and Will thought that they should stop to rest and water the horses. Will voiced that thought to Mandy but he was surprised by her answer.

"We might want to wait to take a respite until after we find out what our visitors have on their minds." She remarked.

Will immediately took a look up at the sky. Sure enough, the hawk was sailing on the breeze directly above them. "So you are talking with the bird again?" Will asked with a smile on his face.

"No, but I have been watching the horizon." Mandy pointed off to their left and Will could see the dust cloud that was rising not too distant from their location.

"Strange that I didn't notice that myself. I guess I was too preoccupied with following the river that I didn't see the obvious danger."

"Or maybe you were preoccupied with watching my rear since I was riding in front of you."

Will's face reddened a little with embarrassment since he had indeed been watching her behind more than he should have been.

Trying to change the subject, Will mused. "I wonder where Caesar has gotten off to."

"I am sure that he is around somewhere. I am hoping that we don't need his help this time but you never know in this country."

The dust cloud kept coming and Will was fairly sure that there was a road of some type off to their left. He reined Prince in that direction. "We might as well go greet our guests." He said as he removed the hammer strap from his sidearm.

He set a course towards where the dust was rising hoping to find the road before the riders reached them. Sure enough, they came on a well-used road. Will was amazed that they had not seen dust clouds before this. It was obvious from the deep wagon ruts that this was the main thoroughfare used regularly. Will looked up the road and could see that at least five riders were coming his way. They were too far in the distance for him to get a good look and he wished he had a pair of binoculars. Of course, he did have the scope on his rifle but he was sure that they might take offense at his sighting his rifle in their direction since they would have no way of knowing he was just trying to get a closer look at them.

He reined his horse off to the right side of the road and motioned for Mandy to do the same. It was not long before the riders came up abreast and reined their horses to a stop. Will reached up and touched the brim of his hat as a form of greeting.

The one in the lead shook his head at the gesture and then tipped his own hat back off his forehead giving Will an even better look at his face. The man was middle-aged judging from the wrinkles under his eyes and the tinge of gray in his hair. A long handlebar mustache made him look somewhat distinguished. He wore a brace of guns each tied down to his legs.

Will kept his eyes on this man not inspecting the other four riders. Will was sure if trouble was to come it would be from the man out front.

Mandy had moved her horse so that she was behind Will and out of the direct line of sight from the group of men.

"Tell your woman to move out from behind you. It makes me nervous when someone is hiding from my view."

"My wife will stay just where she is. She has good reason to stay out of the direct line of sight of men in this part of the country. Now if you have nothing you wish to discuss with me, you might as well ride on."

Will noticed the man's hand begin to move downward towards the gun on his right hip.

"I would not do what you are thinking of." Will's voice was low but with an edge to it.

The hand moved back upwards and away from the gun handle.

"There is no reason to get nervous, feller. If we took a mind to you wouldn't stand much chance against the five of us."

"You may well be right about that," Will replied. "I am not looking for any trouble here but I won't back away from it either. Now, why don't you tell me why you are holding up our travel?"

The man thought for a few seconds before answering. We are looking for three men that came this way recently. Have you seen them by any chance?"

"Sorry but we just intersected this road when we saw your dust cloud. Is there a particular reason you are looking for these gents?"

"They aren't gents as you put it. They are cold-blooded killers. It is a good thing that you didn't cross paths with them. You both would more than likely have been dead but only after they took turns with your wife. They killed a rancher and raped his wife and daughter before cutting their throats."

Will heard Mandy gasp from behind him but he did not turn away from the men in front of him. "I take it you men are some type of lawmen?" Will asked. He did not wait for an answer. "I hope you catch up with them before they hurt any more people."

The man again tipped his hat and then urged his horse into a trot down the road. Will watched the five men ride away before turning to

Mandy. "I didn't want to explain what happened back there. If they do happen upon the bodies, we will be long gone."

"Why didn't you ask where the nearest town is?" Mandy asked him.

"No sense letting them know that we have no idea where we are or where we are going. I figure they are what they say they are but no sense in drawing any more attention to us than is necessary. And besides, if we follow this road in the direction from where they came from we are bound to come in contact with civilization."

With that Will touched Prince's sides with the heel of his boots just enough to let the big horse know they needed to move on.

The sun was rapidly setting behind the hills Will announced to Mandy that it was time for them to seek a campsite for the night. They had left the river hours before and so he needed to find a spot with water and hopefully firewood. Mandy, however, had a different idea.

"Let's push on for another hour or so and hope we come on that civilization you were so sure we are heading towards. If there is a chance of a hot bath and a warm bed versus sleeping under the stars on the hard ground I choose the former."

"And if we don't find a town before it is dark?" Will asked.

"Then I guess we make a cold camp for the night and press on once it gets light. But something tells me that will not be necessary."

Will had come to trust Mandy when she has those types of feelings and so he again urged Prince onward. The sun had completely disappeared beyond the horizon but fortunately, there was enough of a moon so that they could still see the trail they were on. As they topped a rise, they looked down on dim flickering lights that could only be caused by the civilization they had been seeking.

A half-hour later they were passing the first of many wooden structures. The tallest building seemed to be dead center in the town and Will figured that must be the hotel. And as bone-weary, as he was he knew that finding shelter for their horses was paramount. A sign to his left announced that the building was the Sheriff's office but that was the last place that Will wanted to stop and ask for directions. He had his fill of men with stars on their chests.

Presently they came to a watering trough set to one side of the street and they dismounted and led their horses to it so that they could drink their fill. Will bent down and picked up a handful of the water and used it to wash some of the trail dust from his face. He used his neckerchief to wipe the remnants of water and then rinsed out the cloth and tied it back around his neck.

From somewhere Will could hear an old piano playing and he figured that there must be a saloon within a short distance. He listened carefully and then the sounds of raucous laughter reached his ears. Turning to Mandy he handed her a small sack of gold coins and told her to head on down to the hotel and get them a room for the night while he went in search of a livery stable to put up the horses and to make sure they got a measure of grain as well.

She looked at him like he had two heads. "I guess you are forgetting the little rule about women not being allowed to wander around without the guidance of some big strong man?"

"Well, it is such a dumb rule that it is easy to forget, but after all, you have those fake papers with you?"

"Oh, you mean the blank ones? Just because some damned fool Sheriff was fooled by them doesn't mean that the next one will be. No, I think I will stick with you until the horses are stabled and then you and I can mosey on over to the hotel and get comfortable for the night."

They had to walk the full length of the only street before they finally found what they were looking for. The big barn doors were standing open and a sign directed them to put up their own animals and that they could pay when they returned for them. Will quickly stripped the saddles from both horses and while he was looking for some grain for them Mandy began rubbing them down using an old grain sack she found hanging over one of the empty stalls.

It took them a half hour to get the animals settled in for the night and then they started their trek back down the street they had traversed some time ago. They passed the swinging doors of the saloon just as a big man was leaving through them. He looked closely at Will and then gave Mandy more than a casual glance. He was staring so hard that Will was about ready to ask him if he had never seen a woman before when he tipped his hat to Mandy and walked away. He did, however, look back several times making Will feel a little uncomfortable.

They entered the hotel and were gratified to see that the night clerk was at his station behind the counter. He eyed the pair as they walked towards the desk as if it was a strange sight to have a couple walk into his establishment.

"We need a room for the night and a hot bath for my wife if that is not too much trouble." Will announced as he pulled the register towards him and reached for the pen on the desk to sign in."

"I can give you a room alright, Mr. Anderson, is it?" He asked as he looked down at the name on the register. "But it will cost you extra for the bath to be brought up and the tub filled at this time of the night."

Will reached into his saddlebags and produced the small pouch of gold coins. He had some idea of what the currency values were by this time but he simply poured a few coins out onto the counter and waited for the man to take what was required.

The man reached under the counter and Will heard a tinkling of a bell sound. Shortly a youth came from the back room and was instructed to set up a bath in room 203 for the couple. "It will take a few minutes to get ready." The counterman told them. "Perhaps the lad could carry your things up to the room while you have a cup of coffee in our dining area. There might even be some rolls and fruit left from dinner if you are hungry. No extra charge for that."

Will was amazed that anything came complimentary in this new world he had woken up in but he thanked the man and he and Mandy walked into the room that the man had indicated. Will took two cups and filled them with what was clearly coffee that had rewarmed several times. There didn't seem to be any milk or cream left out and he asked if he should request some but Mandy simply took the cup and brought it to her lips and took a sip.

"It will do for tonight." She replied.

They found some rolls which they ate dry. It had been some time since a meager breakfast and anything that filled the void was appreciated. There were also a few apples that Will cut into slices. Coupled with the coffee and bread they were soon sated enough.

Shortly the youth came and announced that everything was prepared for them. He offered to show them the way which Will gratefully accepted handing him a small coin for his troubles. The youth looked at the coin and gave Will a big smile and turned on his heels and started towards the stairs.

"It appears that you made a new friend, big tipper," Mandy announced with a little tinkle of laughter in her voice.

As they entered the room Will noticed that a tub had been set up in the middle of what was not a very large room. A double bed line one wall and a chair and a desk stood against another. There was no curtain for privacy and so Will announced that he was going to check out the saloon while Mandy took her bath.

"Really Will Anderson! You have seen me naked before or is your memory so short that it doesn't go back a few days? I thought that perhaps you would like to share the bath with me."

Will looked at the small tub and shook his head. "I am afraid that two people would not be able to fit in that tub unless they were stacked on top of each other."

Mandy's face lit up as if she had just come down to find presents under the tree on Christmas morning. "Mmm, that sounds pretty good to me. Do you want the top or the bottom?"

Will's face turned beet red as he caught the gist of what she meant. "I think I will leave you to some privacy. I will return and figure out a place to sleep once the tub has been removed."

"And just what is wrong with sleeping in the bed?" She asked as he walked out the door.

Chapter Seventeen - Another Confrontation

Will was still shaking his head as he walked down the steps of the hotel. As he walked out into the street he again noticed the big man that had been paying so much attention to Mandy earlier and he reached down and undid the hammer strap from his pistol as a precaution. With nothing better to do, he walked up the street and pushed through the double doors of the saloon. He stopped just for a minute to view the surroundings before proceeding to the bar and ordering a beer. He had come to realize that in this strange world he was not apt to find a cold beer and he was not disappointed as he took a sip of the bitter warm liquid.

He heard a chair being pushed back from a table. The sound made him a little nervous as it sounded like whoever was getting up was in a hurry to do so. He slowly turned in that direction and noticed that not one man but three were facing him. Each of them had pistols tied down to their legs in the style of gunfighters and Will immediately knew that trouble was heading his way once again.

The one on the far left was the big man he had twice before seen that night.

"Well, if it isn't the big bad gunfighter!" The man exclaimed.

"Do I know you?" Will asked.

"Oh, we met a couple of months back in the town of Salem. It was at a bonfire where we had gathered to roast a witch. And you came along and butted in where you didn't belong. I might not have recognized you if you hadn't still had the witch with you tonight. A man doesn't easily forget that one especially when he has seen her bound and naked."

"You probably should be a little more respectful when you are referring to my wife."

"So she is your wife now. Aren't you afraid of ending up like her last husband? But there is no need for you to worry. You aren't going to be alive in a few minutes in any event. Then we will take a little stroll over to the hotel and truss the witch up and light another fire in the town square. There is nothing as pleasant as watching a witch burn."

"If I was you I would be worried that you might end up like her former husband," Will said.

"Oh, I am sure that the three of us can handle one witch."

"Aren't you forgetting something?" Will asked. "There won't be three of you left alive when the smoke clears."

"Spread out boys." The big man directed.

Just then Will saw someone enter through the saloon doors. He did not dare divert his eyes from the three in front of him and for the first time, he felt a little fear enter his mind. He was in bad enough trouble having to face three guns but if another was joining the party from his side he knew that his jig was up. But then he heard the voice.

"Are you folks starting this party without me?" Jack asked.

"This is not your fight, stranger." The big man declared. "Just step back out those doors and when we have finished with the witch lover here we will let you join us while we roast his woman."

"No, I think that I might just buy into this hand if Will here doesn't mind."

"Not at all Jack. I am glad to have you back my play but what happened to not getting involved?"

"Oh, you know that only applies if I have to kill someone. I am sure I can handle these two without that eventuality while you take care of Henry here."

"So you know who he is?" Will asked.

"Yes, I am acquainted with him. He likes to hurt women and is responsible for several of them going missing over the years. He is all yours I will take care of his friends."

Will didn't have time to reply as he saw Henry's hand flash to his six-shooter. The man was fast, blindingly so but Will was faster. But before he fired Will heard two shots from the doorway. As Will's bullet took Henry in the chest and threw him back against the wall Will whirled to see what had happened to his two friends. They stood shaking their hands as Will took note of the holes in their holsters. Their pistols were still in the leather but Will could see that they would be of no further use to the men.

"I never saw anything like it!" The bartender exclaimed. "Why I never even seen his hands move. One second he was standing there waiting for those two to draw and the next second his guns were in his hands and spitting lead. If you examine those guns I bet you will find that a slug has destroyed the cylinders."

"It is too bad that you had to kill him." Jack stated but I guess as fast as he was you didn't have a lot of choices." Then he turned to the other two. "You gents might want to be moseying along. Will doesn't take kindly to people who threaten his woman." And as quickly as he had entered Jack was gone out into the night.

"Thank you," Will whispered to the blackness beyond the doors.

A hush fell over the bar as Will turned his attention to the two surviving gunmen. "You really should take Jack's advice. It is too late for your friend but you two can still live a while longer if you ride out right now and I never see your faces again."

They did not hesitate and shortly Will heard the sounds of horse's hooves making a quick retreat.

As Will punched out the used cartridge from his gun's cylinder and replaced it with a new one the bartender walked across the room to where the big man lay. The bartender reached down and rummaged through the man's pockets coming out with a handful of banknotes and a few gold coins. He turned and called two of the other patrons over to where he stood. He handed them the coins and asked them if they would carry the man out to the undertakers. "Give him one coin for the burial and keep the other two for yourselves," He directed.

The men were more than eager to obey as one gabbed Henry's feet and the other took him under the shoulders and slowly moved him to the doors of the saloon. The bartender then came over and handed the banknotes to Will. "He won't be needing these any longer."

"Why don't you keep them in case he has a family that comes by looking for him?" And with that Will headed for the doors. He had a sudden need to see a beautiful raven-haired beauty.

Chapter Eighteen - Wedding Bells Ring

As Will walked rapidly back towards the hotel he realized that he probably had known for some time. He was deeply in love with Mandy and it was time that he told her so. As he entered the hotel door he noticed that a good many men were gathered in the lobby and he began to worry that perhaps while he was dealing with Henry and his two cohorts that Mandy had been in danger from another source. Every eye turned and looked at him and a hush came over the crowd as he quickly moved through them to the stairs.

"That is him." One man said in a low voice and Will quickly looked toward the sound to see if he needed to be on guard. But no one seemed to be an immediate threat so Will hurried up the stairs to make sure that Mandy was unharmed.

"He knocked on the door not knowing if Mandy might still be in the tub. When he received no answer to his knock he turned the knob and pushed inward to enter the room. He tried to divert his eyes from the tub in case she might still be soaking but the room was so small that he immediately took in every nook there was. Mandy sat on the edge of the bed with a towel wrapped around her middle. It was just big enough to cover the lower part of her ample breasts and the top part of her legs. She was running a comb through her long black hair and Will could not help but gaze at her natural beauty.

"Thank God, you are alright." He announced as he crossed the room to take her in his arms. As he did so the towel came undone and slid to the floor leaving her naked body pressed against him. For perhaps the first time he was not embarrassed by her nudity and he bent down and pressed his lips to hers."

Mandy had no idea what had taken place to bring this change to her cowboy but she willingly opened her mouth to allow his tongue entrance. She let out a little moan as she greedily sucked on his tongue and felt his manhood come to life through his jeans. When he finally broke the clench she looked up into his eyes and could not believe that she saw a little mist in them.

"So does this mean that you will not be sleeping on the floor tonight?" She asked hopeful for the correct answer.

"Can you wait for me just one more day?" He pleaded.

Mandy was a little disappointed but she figured she had waited this long what was one more day? She gave his earlobe a little nip with her teeth before she agreed and smiled

"May I ask what is going to happen tomorrow that will make a difference in your attitude towards a soft bed versus a hard floor?"

"You can ask but my answering you would spoil the surprise."

The following morning after Will had worked the kinks out of his body, they went down and had breakfast in the dining room of the hotel. Again Will was surprised that there were almost no empty tables, which was strange because he figured that there were more diners than guests staying there.

Every eye turned toward them as they made their way through the room, finally finding a table in the furthest corner. Even when they had seated themselves Will could still see people staring in their direction.

Within seconds of them being seated, a waiter came over to get their order. Will asked him why so many people had shown up and decided to take breakfast in this small room.

"They came to see the fastest gun around of course. And getting a view of the lady that caused the ruckus is a bonus." The man said as he turned over their coffee cups and filled them.

Will now wished that he had not asked since he had not told Mandy about the gunfight the night before. He turned towards her noticing the stringent look on her face. He tried to avoid the subject by picking up his cup and taking a sip from his coffee, but Mandy was having none of that.

"Will Anderson, you better start explaining what he was talking about. Did someone try to kill you again and you just happened to neglect to mention it to me?"

"There was a little altercation in the saloon. But as you can see I am perfectly fine so there isn't much to talk about."

"I think perhaps you better tell me about this little altercation. How many bodies does the coroner have to take care of this morning?"

"Just one. The other two just have sore hands from where an old friend of mine decided to intervene on my behalf. The one that is dead is the big man we saw out in front of the saloon while we were walking by. It seems he was present back in Salem when your former husband tried to burn you at the stake. He wanted a repeat performance done here and I strenuously objected to that idea. He had two friends with him and he told everyone they were going to kill me and then come get you out of the hotel."

"I might have been in a little trouble but Jack showed up and shot the guns out of his friend's hands while I was left to deal with the big man. He was too fast for me to try and wound him. Jack told me that he was responsible for the disappearances of several women and so I don't feel bad that he is no longer in the world."

"And you didn't tell me all this why?" Will could see that Mandy's hand was shaking so much that she was having trouble lifting her coffee cup.

"The hotel lobby was so packed with men when I got back here that I thought something bad had happened to you. I rushed up the stairs and when I saw you safe and sound I was so happy that I didn't want to spoil the moment with this sad tale."

Will reached across the table and took Mandy's hand into his own. He gently stroked it with his thumb wishing that they were not in a public place so that he could take her in his arms and quiet her fears.

Their food arrived and by that time Mandy had overcome the shakes that she had developed when she heard how close she had come to losing this man. She spoke not another word as she ate her breakfast and drank her second cup of coffee.

Will paid the bill and left a generous tip for the waiter and then asked Mandy if she would go with him to buy a special item. She agreed but tried to pressure him to tell her what the item was. He smiled into her eyes but refused to spoil the secret he had planned.

They walked out on a bright sunlit day. Everywhere they went people were looking at them and whispering things that they could not hear but that Will had a good idea about. He held her hand as they crossed the street guiding her around puddles of water and piles of horse droppings. She was totally confused when He stopped in front of a dressmaker's shop.

Will opened the door and ushered her inside. He left her to wander by herself among the racks of clothing that had been made for other people or so she assumed. Will was only gone a short time when he returned with the proprietor of the shop. She looked at Mandy and said. "I think I have just the right dress for you. I may have to take the hem in just a little bit but it should be fine."

Again Mandy looked at Will and demanded that he tell her what this was all about. He merely said that she would know soon enough and to follow the woman who owned the shop.

When Mandy finally caught up with the woman she was shocked to see her holding up a long white satin dress. Mandy had never seen anything so beautiful in her life and a tear came to her eye when she realized what Will might have in his mind.

"I wanted you to have a dress that was almost as beautiful as you are for your wedding. That is if you will have me?"

She flew into his arms and mashed her lips firmly against his. He was almost out of breath before she finally settled back on the flats of her feet and stepped back to look into his eyes. "You realize that women have no choice in these matters?"

"Well, Amanda, you have a choice. So tell me, will you marry me and make me the happiest man on the face of the earth."

"I will marry you Will Anderson, but whether that will make you happy only time will tell."

While Mandy was being fitted Will went shopping for the other necessary element of a marriage. He did not find precisely what he was looking for because apparently wedding rings were not something that was given very often. He did, however, find a couple of gold rings that he thought would fit the bill, purchased them, and slipped them into his pocket.

An hour later, Will and Amanda were sitting in the parlor of the local religious leader. Will had explained to him that he wished for him to preside over a marriage ceremony. The man had appeared shocked at the request. "I have never presided over such a ceremony. Normally I am only called on to witness when a man takes a woman under his protection. There isn't much of a ceremony involved, just the signing of some papers and my witnessing them."

Will thought for a few minutes and then asked for paper and a pen. He spent a long time writing out what he remembered from his former life when he had been united to his previous wife. When he was finally finished he handed the paper to the preacher and told him that this was what a normal wedding ceremony might sound like.

The preacher read the document and then looked at Will strangely. "You do realize that men do not ask women if they want to marry them. Women have no choice in the matter. Normally they are sold by their parents to a man willing to provide them protection in exchange for their absolute obedience."

"Well, I prefer to have my wife marry me because she loves me not because I paid for her. Can you perform the service and make out the proper papers so that everything is legal and binding?"

"I can and I will but I think this event should be witnessed by the bulk of the townspeople. This will be something that is talked about for years to come." With that, he left Will and Amanda seated in his parlor as he rushed out to rally the town's folks.

It was late in the afternoon, under a flower-covered gazebo that Will and Amanda stood facing each other holding hands while perhaps a hundred men, women, and children served as witnesses. The preacher began. "Dearly beloved, we have gathered here today to witness the joining of Will Anderson and Amanda Wilkes in holy matrimony." A hush fell over the crowd as he got to the part, "Amanda Wilkes will you take this man to be your lawfully wedded husband, to have and to hold from this day forward, for richer or poorer, in good times and bad, keeping yourself only unto him for as long as you both shall live."

Amanda was all smiles but had a little tear in her eye as she affirmed that yes indeed she would. The same question was asked of Will and with happiness flooding his heart he declared that yes he would.

Then the final surprise was sprung as he produced two gold rings from his pocket, one for his third finger left hand and one that he prayed would fit Amanda's.

The preacher then read the written lines about sealing the marriage with the rings and then pronounced them husband and wife to the cheers of every woman in the crowd but to the dismay of many of the men.

"Never before have I asked a woman whether she would agree to marry a man." He announced.

"Well, perhaps this will start a new tradition," Will said as he shook the man's hand.

"I certainly hope so." Announced the preacher's woman.

Then as the crowd opened up so that the couple could walk from the gazebo, Will received a surprise of his own. They were led to a huge feast that had been quickly put together. Music began to play and Will led his new bride to an open spot of lawn and took her into his arms and led her through her first waltz. Even when they stumbled a couple of times she still gazed into his eyes with a love that would last forever.

A spot had been saved for them at the head of a long table. But before they could eat every woman in attendance had to come up to Mandy and give her a hug and thank her for bringing such a wonderful new tradition into their lives.

That night as Will lay in his wife's arms savoring the afterglow of the best sex he had ever experienced he thanked the God that he had so often denied for the precious gift of this woman beside him.

Epilogue

Will and Amanda had ridden out of the town side by side. No two people had ever been happier to be together. They now had the proper papers to prove to everyone that they belonged together and no one had the right to interfere with their travels together.

In due time they found a spot at the base of a tall mountain that had plenty of grass and water where they could raise cattle and a few horses that had previously run wild but that Will with the help of his wife had managed to break and domesticate. Caesar was still with them and Will had even been able to hire a small crew of men to help around the ranch he had established.

Knowing that there were still dangerous men in the world they had built their house inside a large cave and had constructed an almost impregnable door across the entrance. Over time that house became home to not only Will and Amanda but to two of the most beautiful daughters that any union had ever produced.

Then one day while his men were out working in the fields, trouble came. Mandy knew the riders were coming even before Will heard the snorting of the horses and the rattle of their sabers. Mandy urged him to come inside their home where he would be safe but Will knew that his girl's safety depended on him being outside where he must face the trouble head-on. He forced Mandy to take the girls and barricade themselves behind the big door. But before she went into the haven of safety she sent Caesar to get help.

As the first rider came into view, Will recognized him as being a Calvary officer and he hoped that his fears were unfounded. There were eleven other riders following him and each one had a long saber hanging from their side and a pistol on the other hip.

As they pulled up in front of Will the leader announced that they needed water for their horses and some food for his men. Will pointed down the trail a way and told the officer that there was a stream there that would provide water for both their horses and their use. He further told them that they were welcome to cut a steer out of his herd of cattle so that they could butcher it for meat.

The man looked at him and said. "That is all well and good but how about some women for our use?"

Will lowered his hand close to the butt of his revolver wishing that he had more than six rounds of ammunition to use. "There are no women here." He announced.

"You are not a very good liar, mister. We have been watching you and your lovely wife and daughters for the past hour and we mean to have them."

Will knew that if he was to survive that he needed some distraction. He figured he could probably kill three or four before they got him but that would still leave 8 or 9 for Mandy to deal with.

The officer then ordered his sergeant to take two troopers to go bring the women out of the structure. As the three troopers turned and dismounted and headed up the walk to the house, a shotgun blast sounded followed closely by two rifle shots. Will immediately knew that the odds had been cut down by three and he threw himself behind the water trough that stood in the middle of the yard. He drew and fired while he was still in the air and the officer that led the troop slumped from his saddle. Guns erupted all around him and bullets splashed water in his face and kicked up dust beside him. He fired again and heard a groan of pain and knew that his projectile had found its mark.

He felt a pain in his side and another in his left arm. And still, he took aim and fired, again and again, each time hitting his target. When he heard his gun click on empty he was sure that he had finally lost a battle, something that he had been sure would never happen.

But the then shotgun roared again and so did the two rifles. And then all went black as Will slumped to the ground.

It was all dark when Will finally opened his eyes and he was afraid that he had again been sent into that cave to start again with some new life. That was a terrible thought because the only life he wanted to live was the one he had with Mandy and his daughters. But then he felt a wet rag being wiped across his face. He reached out and was happy to feel his hands make contact with a huge ball of fur. Caesar whined to alert Mandy that Will was awake and she quickly got up and lit a lantern and brought it over to him. She could see good color in his face and she knew that the fever had broken. "Thank God, you are awake." She said as she lay down beside him and put her lips to his.

Will smiled. "Yes and Thank God that you are alright as well. And the girls?"

"They are just fine although it took them a while to get over the fact that they had to kill those men so that they would not hurt their father anymore. And incidentally, another troop of soldiers came through the next day. But these were real soldiers that had been sent to capture the renegades that we had to kill. They said they were going to spread the word about what had happened here and they were quite sure that anyone seeking trouble would think twice before seeking it here."

Will and Amanda lived untroubled lives from that day forward. Oh, they had to deal with all the same things that the rest of us do, storms and droughts, cold and heat, good times and bad. But Will never had to draw his gun again to protect those he loved. And that was all he expected from life. But he never forgot to thank God for allowing him to have a second life that was so much more fulfilling than his first one.

He knew that his life was ending again but he was happy as he bounced a little girl on each knee. They were his great-grandchildren and they loved him dearly. "Tell us a story, Grandpa." They begged with joy in their voices.

"What do you want to hear, girls?" He asked.

"Tell us again about the lights on the VCR and remind us what a VCR is?

The end.

I really hope that you enjoyed reading this book as much as I did writing it. I want to thank Greg Baylor for his encouraging me to write this sequel to "I Wish I Were a Cowboy". Without that encouragement, I might have left the story unfinished

If you have questions, comments, or suggestions you would like to share with me please do not hesitate to write me directly. My email address is: waynesimmes@yahoo.com

Another book you might like to read:

https://www.smashwords.com/books/view/1028323

The Devil
The Ghost And
Will Anderson
By Wayne Simmes